Spies in Disguise

Kate Scott was born in London. She has lived in Hong Kong, Paris, Scotland, and two tiny villages in France. She now lives in Dorset with her husband and two children.

Kate writes children's books, children's television programs, radio plays, and poetry. She's had lots of different jobs but now she makes up stories—the best job in the world.

She likes drawing, dancing, reading, and 1940s films. She hates raw tomatoes and being tickled.

Sometimes her children read what she's writing and give her advice on how to make it better.

Spies in Disguise

BOY IN TIGHTS

KATE SCOTT

Sky Pony Press
New York

Dedicated to the memory of Margaret Carey:
a dear friend, a warm wit,
a generous spirit,
an outstanding talent.

Copyright © 2013 Kate Scott
Illustration copyright © 2013 Clare Elsom
First published in 2013 by Piccadilly Press, London

First Sky Pony Press edition, 2016

Sky Pony Press books may be purchased in bulk at special discounts for sales promotion, corporate gifts, fund-raising, or educational purposes. Special editions can also be created to specifications. For details, contact the Special Sales Department, Sky Pony Press, 307 West 36th Street, 11th Floor, New York, NY 10018 or info@skyhorsepublishing.com.

Sky Pony® is a registered trademark of Skyhorse Publishing, Inc.®, a Delaware corporation.

Visit our website at www.skyponypress.com.

10 9 8 7 6 5 4 3 2 1

Library of Congress Cataloging-in-Publication Data is available on file.

Cover design by Simon Davis
Cover illustration credit Clare Elsom

Print ISBN: 978-1-63450-689-2
Ebook ISBN: 978-1-63450-690-8

Printed in the United States of America

Spies in Disguise

Chapter 1

Dan McGuire—secret agent, supreme genius— would never put up with this. Dan McGuire is cooler than ice cubes. Dan McGuire decides his own bedtime. Dan McGuire would give my mom one look and she'd crumble like cake.

Unfortunately, Dan McGuire isn't here.

Dan McGuire only exists in books.

I've just walked through the door—I haven't even put my backpack down—when Mom hits me with it. I came home looking forward to getting a stack of sandwiches and settling down in front of the TV. Instead, I've been ambushed by Mom and Dad in the hall.

"We're moving—*today?*" I repeat after her. "You're joking." I scan her face for telltale twitches—any signs that she's trying to be funny.

Not even a nostril flare. In fact, she's looking pretty scary.

"I'm not joking."

No explanations, no apologies. No preparation, no packing, no realtors. No discussions, no warning. No nothing.

"We can't move just like that!" I say.

"No time for drama," Dad replies. "We need to get a move on."

I take a deep breath—I need to talk to them carefully, in case they're not just crazy, but they're actually dangerous. "We can't just *leave.*"

"We'll tell you everything when we get there, Joe," Dad says. His voice is low and urgent, like he's in a disaster film at the point where they tell you the volcano's about to blow.

That's when I see the two suitcases and small bag by the front door.

Maybe you shouldn't argue when the volcano's about to blow.

"What about my stuff?" If they've packed for me there's no way they haven't left something important behind.

"Joe . . ." Mom starts.

"Let him go, Zelia," Dad says.

Mom taps her watch. "Thirty seconds."

I run. I have the washing-machine-stomach feeling I get before anything big happens. The problem is, I don't know if this is the start of an adventure—like when Ryan Jackson's parents decided to move the family to Australia—or the beginning of a nightmare—like when Connor Forsey had to have two teeth pulled after putting toothpaste on his tongue instead of using a toothbrush for a year.

Upstairs, I look around my room—at all my soccer posters, at my ancient washed-out comforter with the miniature planes on it that I've never let Mom throw out, at the pile of Dan

McGuire Secret Agent books I know by heart. Wherever we're going, it can't be for long if they've left all my stuff. The thought calms me down. Sort of.

I grab my soccer ball from the closet and my gym bag from the floor (how could they *not* have packed my soccer ball?) and stuff in as many Dan McGuire books as I can. I go back down the stairs three at a time.

In the hall, Mom grabs my arm as I turn toward the front door. "Not that way, Joe."

A cell phone rings once and then cuts off.

"That's our signal," Dad says. "We've got to get out of here—now!"

"Here." Mom shoves a ski mask at me as Dad picks up the suitcases. "Put this on."

"You want me to look like a thief?"

"Just do as your mom says," Dad snaps. Dad hardly ever gets annoyed—what's going on?!

I tug on the too-small ski mask until my head's trapped in the woolen vice. My eyes are bugging out of the tiny eyeholes. This could be one of those TV programs where they convince some idiot that something incredible is happening. Then the idiot has to pretend to laugh when it turns out it's all a practical joke.

I hope I'm not the idiot.

"Come on," Mom says, thrusting the small bag at me.

We leave the house the back way. There's a long, shiny black car parked in the driveway. The car beeps and Mom and Dad slide in, gesturing for me to get in the back. It's sleek, new, clean. Nothing like the car we used to have—the one Dad nicknamed Snack for Scrap.

"On the move," Dad murmurs. He's talking into the smallest phone I've ever seen. It's silver, about the size of a credit card and almost as thin.

Mom starts the car and eases out into the street. Seconds later we're swinging onto the main road.

I lean forward, putting my face between the two front seats. Dad points his phone at the dashboard and clicks. Panels slide back to reveal dozens of tiny red and green flashing lights, buttons, and switches. A large blue screen in the dashboard shows a squiggle of roads, and a little red dot blinks along one of them. I guess that little red dot is us.

I touch the seats—they're soft and smooth instead of rough and sticky and covered in crumbs. Why couldn't Mom and Dad have picked me up from school in *this*?

"Sit back, sweetheart." Mom glances into the rear-view mirror. "And tighten your seatbelt."

Before I can reply, Mom makes a sudden gear change and I'm thrown against the back of my seat. The car's wheels screech as she takes a hard right, then a left, then another right. I grab hold of the door handle as I'm swung from side to side. This is *Mom* driving? The woman who thinks you shouldn't drive faster than someone with a walker can walk?

Mom swerves around another corner.

"Are we in a car chase?" I manage to ask, after my face meets the back of the front seat for the third time.

"We'll talk about it later, Joe. You all right back there?" Dad sounds cheery now, almost but not quite like the dad I remember from before today. "You can take the ski mask off now. Relax."

Relax? But I pull off the ski mask. We're on the highway now and Mom's really putting her foot down. She zips through to the fast lane and stays there. If we were in a Grand Prix race Mom would *definitely* be winning.

This is totally awesome!

Dad jabs at the buttons on the dashboard. It's obvious he knows the car's controls back to front. The dad who used to fumble with the gas cap and stall the car on hills is gone.

As we whip along the highway, speeding past the kind of cars I used to watch speeding past us, I can't help wishing my best friend Eddie could see me. Up until today, Mom and Dad have been cup-of-tea-and-a-cookie-in-front-of-the-TV, ordinary parents. I watch the red dot pulse across the screen as Mom weaves through the lanes and Dad jabs at buttons like a professional computer hacker. There's no way I can call them ordinary now.

All of a sudden, Mom and Dad are strangers.

Chapter 2

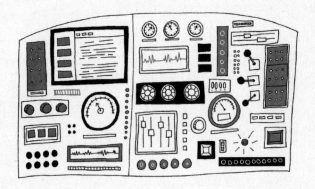

I've just launched into a new round of questions when a piercing beep sounds and *CODE ES3503* scrolls across the top of the screen. A green dot appears behind our red dot.

Dad flicks a bunch of switches with the tips of his fingers and a video image of a car flashes up on screen. "It's a Corsa. Red. License plate NES 160. It's getting close."

"Not for long, it isn't," Mom says. She guns the engine and swings back over to the fast lane.

My seatbelt cuts into my chest as we surge forward. Mom zips from lane to lane. We're going so fast the streetlights blur but the gap between the red and the green dot widens as Mom speeds ahead. On a "this is amazing" scale of one to ten, this is *eleven*.

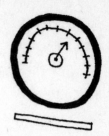

Dad's phone beeps and he reads a message. "Back-up's installing some roadworks. If you can keep up the speed for another four minutes we'll be out of danger."

Mom laughs. "No problem."

Dad used to call Mom the Couch Potato Princess. Now she's acting like a speed demon. *Where's my mom gone?!*

I'm pushed even further back into my seat as Mom puts her foot to the floor. We whip by signs so fast I can't even read them.

The green dot slows to a stop and then disappears from the edge of the screen. "We're in the clear," Dad tells us.

"Excellent," Mom says. "I won't even have to double back." She slows down—slightly—and takes the next exit. A few minutes later we come to a stop.

I peer out of the tinted window. We're parked in front of a squat, dirty brown building. It looks like an enormous toad. A small yellow neon sign is flashing STACEY'S SELF-SERVICE MOTEL.

"I'll check us in." Mom cuts the engine.

I notice a black iron fire escape zigzagging up the side of the building. In *Dan McGuire Meets the Agent of Doom*, Dan is chased down fifty floors of a fire escape, taking the last flight in one leap. At this point, I wouldn't be surprised if Mom and Dad do something similar.

Mom slips out of the car, closing the door gently behind her. She glances from left to right and then walks up to a steel panel next to the motel's front door and presses some buttons.

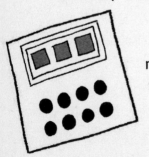

"What's happening?"

Dad ignores me. He's taken his miniature phone out of his pocket. "First destination," he says into it.

As Dad tucks the phone out of sight, Mom beckons us from the door, which is now open. Dad's out of the car before I've even undone my seatbelt. I didn't know he had it in him to move that fast.

"Come on." Dad's holding the small bag and is glancing around the parking lot as if he's watching out for something. I keep close to him—I have a feeling I don't want to find out what that something is.

Mom and Dad bundle me through the door and more or less push me along the hall. It smells of mold and cat pee and is painted a green that reminds me of school. Not in a good way. All the room doors are a matte gray, with a keypad next to them. The person who designed this place probably does prisons and schools as well.

We stop at a door at the end of the hall, next to a fire exit. Mom jabs at the keypad, and the door gives a soft click. She sticks her head in, looks around, then yanks at my arm to pull me inside.

"Hey!"

"Shhh," Dad hisses from behind me.

Once we're inside, the door closes softly behind us. To the left there's a double bed with a dirty orange cover and another single bed by the window in front of us. The curtains are made from the same grubby orange material covering the beds. The smell of mold and cat pee is really strong now.

Whatever's happened to Mom and Dad must be bad if this is the kind of place we'll be staying in. I go over to the single bed and sit down. The mattress sags so far it almost touches the ground. I'm not sure I'll be able to get up.

Then Mom and Dad start acting weird again—or weirder.

Dad goes over to the window and draws the curtains. Then he picks up and peers at the

lamps, examines the earpiece of the room's phone, checks under the beds. Mom takes the drawers out of the side table and examines the inside. She turns the drawers over before sliding them back in.

Eventually they seem to get tired of ransacking the room.

"Okay." Dad sits down on

the double bed. "Time to talk."

Mom sits down next to him and clasps her hands around her knees.

I sit up as straight as I can on the sagging bed. "Are we running away from the police?"

"No!" Mom's got some nerve looking shocked at my suggestion.

"We haven't done anything wrong," Dad says.

"You said we're in trouble," I point out.

"We are, but it's because of other people." Dad draws out his words as if testing them to see how much they give away. "The thing is, I'm not a political consultant. And your mother isn't a computer programmer."

"We're spies," Mom says.

"What?!" I don't know what I was expecting, but it definitely wasn't *this*.

Dad glares at Mom.

She shrugs. "We had to tell him."

"I was planning on leading up to it a bit," he says.

"HANG ON!"

Mom and Dad jump.

"*Spies?*" Dad doesn't look anything like James Bond—any of them—and Mom . . .

I stop and consider their black clothes, the small black case, and the drawn curtains. I think of the fast, sleek car outside.

Yeah, they look exactly like spies.

"We've been working undercover for so long we didn't think we'd have to move again," Mom says. "We moved all the time before you were born."

I open my mouth. Then I shut it again.

"I know it's a bit of a shock, but we're on the run," Mom says, reaching down to tug at her boots. She pulls one off and fiddles with the heel. It pops open and she empties out a small metal object. She tosses it to Dad. He catches it neatly with one hand.

"Sensor," Dad says, as if that's an explanation.

Dad gets up and sticks the object in the center of the door, where it winks at us with a small green light.

"You're not kidding, are you?"

"No. We're not," Dad says.

"You're really spies?"

"We're really spies," Mom says.

"And we're not going home."

"I'm sorry, Joe," Dad says. "But our covers have been blown. We're going to have to go somewhere else and become new people for a while."

"How long for? You mean, *forever*?"

Dad crouches down in front of me and puts his hand on my shoulder. "We might move on again, but we can never go back to where we were, no."

"It's just too dangerous," Mom says, her voice soft. "Believe me, we wouldn't be doing this unless we had to."

I gaze at the swirly green and orange carpet. On the one hand, I'm never going back to my old life again. There's my friend Eddie—I'll miss Eddie. And I really wish I'd packed *all* of my Dan McGuire book collection.

But on the other hand, I can expect car chases and spy gadgets and cool black outfits. I can expect the kind of stuff that happens to Dan McGuire on a daily basis. Carbonated drinks by swimming pools, traveling on high-speed trains and planes in first class, having the FBI shake your hand and say, "Good work, son." Maybe there's even a five-a-side team for all the kids of spies. Or maybe we'll have to move to Brazil on diplomatic spy business and I'll get talent-spotted by my favorite soccer team of all time—Santos. Maybe the team will all sign my shirt.

So long, Eddie.

"This is going to be *great!*"

Dad coughs. "Yeah. The thing is . . ." He trails off, glancing at Mom.

Mom pushes her hair behind her ear. "The thing is, our new cover story means a few changes."

"Quite big changes." Dad doesn't seem to want to look me in the eye.

"A new house. A new school." Do they think I don't get it?

"Yes," Mom says. But she looks awkward, too.

Before I can ask why, a low, metallic voice speaks. "Subject eight yards away."

Mom and Dad swivel towards the door. The sensor is flashing blips of red light. "Subject six yards away." I realize the voice is coming from the sensor.

Dad pulls the curtains and opens the window. Mom swishes the bag along the floor toward Dad. Dad picks it up and fishes out a coil of metal rope with a hook at the end of it. He attaches the hook to the windowsill and drops the cable out of the window. Then he gestures me toward it.

"Out there?" I whisper.

Dad nods. "Wait until I tell you to go," he whispers back. He holds his finger up to his lips.

The metallic voice speaks again, this time more softly. "Subject less than two feet away."

That's pretty cool, a gadget that knows when to lower its voice.

Mom ducks into the bathroom and turns the faucet on in the tub.

There's a sharp knock on the door.

Mom detaches the sensor from the door and slips it into her pocket.

Another knock.

I really hope Mom and Dad are good at their job.

Mom waves to Dad, who bends down and picks up the boot she'd taken off and flings it across the room. She catches it neatly and pulls it back on as there's a third rap on the door.

"Yes?" Mom shouts over the noise of the running water.

From the other side of the door there's a deep voice. "Room service."

"I think there's been a mistake. I didn't order any room service."

"No mistake. It's on the house," the deep voice says.

Dad pulls me close, whispering in my ear. "I'll give you a leg up. Go and get in the red car next to the space we were in."

"But that's not—"

"Have to keep them guessing," Dad tells me.

"Sure." I do my best to act as if I'm always being asked to jump out of windows and into strange cars.

"Fast as you can. Here are the keys." He pushes them into my hand. "Press the button on the keyring when you get near it."

"Where are you going?" Blood's rushing in my ears.

"We'll be right behind you," Dad says. "Now *go*."

He hoists me up and almost in the same movement, I'm sliding down the wire to the asphalt below. I land and race toward the red car, holding out the keyring and jabbing the button. The car beeps and the driver's side door swings open. As I dive in, the engine starts up by itself. I look back and see Mom and Dad crossing the parking lot, running fast. I scramble into the back seat and click my seatbelt. I've got the hang of this enough to know I'll need to be strapped in tight. Within a second of them getting in, we're screeching out of the lot. Mom speeds down a series of narrow winding lanes. There aren't any streetlights and we're skidding around sharp bends in the pitch black, but Mom doesn't let that slow her down.

"Well, that was an amateur move," Mom says. "Didn't even have anyone watching the window."

"Not completely amateur." Dad taps the screen where a new green dot is blinking behind our red one.

Mom sighs. "Oh well. I guess that's to be expected." She sounds like she's talking about a bad weather forecast, not about being chased by enemy spies!

She revs the engine and we screech around another corner. "Hang on."

I always thought a high-speed escape would be exciting, but actually it's making me feel a bit sick. My face is squashed flat against the window as Mom takes a spectacularly sharp corner. I manage to speak out of the side of my mouth. "Are they coming after us?"

"They can try." Mom sounds cheerful, as if she likes the idea of a real chase. My old mom didn't even like putting her foot down on bumper cars. It's going to take a while to get used to this new version.

"We weren't going to stay at the motel for long anyway," Dad calls back to me. "It's what we call a destination decoy."

"We weren't going to stay there?" It's been a long day. I'm finding it hard to keep up.

"Of course not!" Mom says. "I wouldn't be caught dead sleeping on those dirty sheets!" Mom spins the wheel to turn another corner.

"They won't catch us, will they?" I don't want to meet Mom and Dad's enemies without having some training first. And a couple of their gadgets.

"Don't worry. Your mom's an old hand at this. Usually we wouldn't have expected them to find us so quickly, but they were slightly more ahead of the game than we expected."

"Not *that* ahead of the game," Mom says. "Honestly—room service? As if!"

"You don't get room service in a self-service motel, do you?"

"Exactly."

The gap between the two dots widens. Once the dot disappears from the screen, Mom heads back to the highway (which at least means no more swerving around bends). Then she sweeps into the fast lane and overtakes any car that has the nerve to get in front of her.

"Back-up have tracked them down," Dad murmurs to Mom.

I lean back and watch the cars swooshing past. Normal cars with their normal people on their way to normal places.

Not like my family. We're spies on the run—in serious danger.

How FANTASTIC is that?

Chapter 3

Mom and Dad are sitting opposite me on the edge of their bed. They keep shifting their positions and glancing at each other.

We arrived at the second motel in the middle of the night—the room had sheets that Mom approved of. Even the sensor liked it—it stayed silent for the rest of the night, or what was left of it. Now it's morning but I could do with at least another four hours of sleep. I push up my eyelids with my fingers and yawn loudly. Maybe they'll get the hint and let me go back to bed.

"You have to understand, we need to change our identities," Dad starts. "If we're going to stay safe it's vital that no one can recognize us."

"They could be watching us, following us, at any time." Mom glances at the sensor and I shiver, even though the room is hot and stuffy.

I really get it now—my old life is gone: Eddie; the soccer team; my teacher, Mr. Burnside; Saturday mornings in the park; nice, ordinary parents. It's all gone for good.

Mom takes a breath. "You remember Cousin Andrea?"

"Yeah, of course I remember her," I say, wondering what Cousin Andrea's got to do with anything. Cousin Andrea sometimes comes over to see Mom and Dad. She's always in a state about something and it's always "private." Mom and Dad have to have long whispered conversations with her in the kitchen. The only good thing about it is that they send me to the fast food restaurant to keep me out of the way. I guess that's gone now, too.

"Cousin Andrea," Mom says, "isn't exactly what she seems." She tugs at her ear. "Cousin Andrea is actually Special Agent Andrew."

"What?!"

"She's a man, Joe," Dad says. "She—I mean, he—is an undercover agent."

I think back to all the times I've seen Cousin Andrea. I picture those big hands, the shapeless dresses, the thick, hairy legs. My mind races.

There's a reason they're telling me this.

And I see the expression in their eyes and I understand what that reason is.

No. They won't really say it. They can't! They wouldn't dare.

"It's often a part of going undercover," Dad says.

"You're starting your new school as a girl," Mom says quickly.

If my eyes were laser beams I'd be burning holes in Mom's face. "No. Way."

"Yes," says Mom.

"Absolutely NO WAY!"

"It won't be hard to remember your new name because it's so like your old one—Josephine," Mom goes on. "So, that's one good thing."

Josephine?! A *good* thing?!

"We can call you Josie for short. That's pretty."

"You can stop right there." I give Mom the laser glare again. "I'm not doing it."

Mom lasers me back. "Yes, you are."

"Honestly, we feel really bad about this." Dad looks like he means it, but what good is that?

"Why can't I change my hair? Have a different name? You can call me anything you like. I'll take Reginald! Brian! Nigel! I don't care, just don't make me be a girl!"

Mom's eyebrows dart up in warning.

I lower my voice. "Please."

"Think about it. It makes sense. Most people wouldn't believe it's possible to disguise a boy as a girl," Mom says. "They'd think that no boy would agree to it."

"THAT'S BECAUSE THEY'RE RIGHT!"

 "So, when they're searching for a family of three with a son, your disguise as a girl will be what keeps us safe," she finishes up.

"We have to throw them off our trail, Joe," Dad says, spreading out his hands.

"Then why can't I stay behind? I could stay with someone. Anyone!"

Mom and Dad become very still.

"Don't you want to be with us?" Mom says, and for the first time she sounds not businesslike, not like a spy or a stranger, but like my mom. My mom when she's upset.

"Yes, of course I do," I say quickly. Just not as a girl.

"We wouldn't be asking you to do this if we weren't in danger," Dad says.

"A lot of danger," Mom adds.

For Dan McGuire, danger means escaping on a jet or in a high-speed train or in a Lexus LFA. Apparently, for me it means prancing around in a dress.

But if we're in real trouble . . . I have to at least consider helping. I'd be saving Mom and Dad from the enemy.

"How long would I have to do this for?"

"Well," Dad says, "until we're sure we haven't been tracked to our new location. Three to six months, say."

"Three to six months! Three to six *months*!" They have got to be kidding!

27

"Calm down," Mom says. "It probably won't be that long anyway. It's just until things go back to normal. And until back-up tracks down the people after us."

"We wouldn't ask if it wasn't serious." Dad pulls at his beard. "We're only doing this for your own protection."

"My own protection!"

"Stop repeating everything we say," Mom says. "Honestly, can't you think of it as kind of fun?"

There's no way Dan McGuire would go down without a fight. It's time to make myself understood. Danger or not, there are some lines you don't cross.

"I am never, ever, *ever* going to wear a dress."

Fifteen minutes later, I'm standing in front of the mirror in the tiny bathroom. My scalp itches. Bright yellow hair hangs down around my face like shiny spaghetti. I reach up to scratch.

"Don't do that! You'll make the wig wonky and give the game away."

"But it's really itchy!"

"Well, do it *carefully* then," Mom says. "I'm sorry we can't curl and dye your hair but it's too short. It has to be a wig."

"This. Is. My. Worst. Nightmare."

Mom just smiles and smooths down my wig.

Some of the boys at my school have friends who are girls. I'm not one of them. How can I pretend to be something I don't even understand?

The Santos team back in Brazil are never going to sign my shirt now.

"Now the dress," Mom says. "Arms up."

I stick my arms up in the air as if I'm being arrested. Except being arrested would be better— at least I'd be allowed to wear pants.

To make things even worse, it's a pink dress—a pink dress with *frilly* parts. It's the kind of dress my sister would wear. If I had a sister. Mom slips it over my head.

"It's like wearing a tent! My legs are freezing!"

"Then put on the tights." Mom hands them to me. "They'll cover them up." She sighs. "Pity you developed hairy legs so early. Apart from that and your feet, you've got a lovely feminine build."

"Do you mind?! Hairy legs are normal, if you're a boy!" It's true; I got hair on my legs before any other boy in my school. And yes, I have bigger feet than anyone else in my class. But that was never a problem—until now.

The tights are like two snakes hanging down from a gaping mouth—and they're about to eat my legs alive. I hold them at arm's length. "How am I supposed to put these on?"

"Don't be silly," Mom says. "One leg at a time."

I lift up one leg and make a stab at putting my foot in the large hole. I get it in the large part but then lose my balance as I push my toes further down one of the legs. I fall over with the snakes tangled around my ankles. "This is so *stupid.*"

"Oh, for heaven's sake." She pulls me up to standing and shows me how to roll each leg up so I can stick my toes in the foot of the tights. Eventually, I manage it.

The tights itch my thighs and it's still drafty under the dress. How do girls cope with it? Anything could crawl under there. And where are the pockets?

"You'll get used to it," Mom says. She swivels me around. Looking in the mirror is like turning to see an awful accident. You don't want to but you can't help yourself.

I'm the ugliest girl I've ever seen.

"I. Look. Ridiculous."

Dad appears at the door. "How are we getting along? Oh. I see." Dad's got a trying-not-to-laugh look on his face. "Honestly, Joe, it's not that bad."

"No. It's worse."

"Well, I think you're very . . . pretty." Mom adjusts my wig.

"Pretty!"

There's a strangled sound from Dad.

"Get yourself under control," Mom tells him.

I grit my teeth. "You know, lots of girls wear pants."

"I did tell your dad that," Mom says, "but I'm afraid he did all the clothes ordering while I was out."

"There's no way we can risk pants yet," Dad says. "Not until you're really convincing as a girl. People believe what they're presented with. We have to present them with nothing but girl."

"Well, anyway, Josie," Mom says, "your dad and I will get our new disguises together and then we can go."

"You don't need to call me that *now*."

"We may as well get used to it as soon as possible." She's wearing what I already think of as her Serious Spy look. "It'll only take one slip-up for the secret to be out, and that's all the enemy needs to find us."

Even Dad's stopped smiling. "It's really not a joke."

He's telling me!

Mom rummages in her bag and pulls something out. "This might make you feel better. We know you've been wanting a cell phone for years—"

"I wanted it to call my *friends*. The ones we're *leaving*."

Mom ignores me. "So, we got you a reward for being so understanding," she says, placing a slim phone in my hand.

"Who says I'm being understanding? I'm only doing this so we don't get caught." But since I've wanted a cell phone since roughly forever, I give her a smile, then I look down to check it out.

It's bright pink.

Chapter 4

In every Dan McGuire book, there's a True Stories section about real-life spies. While I'm waiting for Mom and Dad, I remember that in *Dan McGuire and the Code-Cracker*, the true story is about Lea de Beaumont, the alias of Chavalier d'Éon—a man who dressed up as a woman so he could spy on the Empress of Russia.

This does not make me feel any better.

Half an hour later, with help from some extra high heels and a bottle of hair dye, Mom's a tall redhead in a stylish dress and jacket. Dad's beard is gone, and he's wearing a suit. It's like they've been abducted by aliens and replaced with brand new versions of their old selves. I notice *their* new covers don't involve them being embarrassed to death. Only yesterday I was looking forward to showing off one day about having cool spy parents. Now I wish everything was how it used to be.

Dad plucks the still-quiet sensor from the door and chucks it to Mom. "Well, we better get on the road, girls; we've got a way to go."

He's talking about us. Girls. Mom and I are the "girls." For a second I can't breathe.

Out in the hall, I have to learn to walk all over again. The tights make my legs feel prickly so I waddle, but then Mom tells me to stop walking like a cowboy. The dress makes *swish-swish* sounds against my legs, and because there are no pockets to plunge my hands into, my arms hang down by my sides like an orangutan. My new long hair tickles my cheeks. It's a nightmare come to life.

When Dan McGuire went undercover in *Dan McGuire—Stunt Spy* he got to pretend to be a stunt man for a film star and do things like leap across seventy bikes using a motor-powered scooter. But there's no way Josie is going to be leaping across anything. Not in these tights.

Outside, Mom leads us through the parking lot to a dark green car.

"Another one?"

As we're driving away from the motel Mom explains. "We have to switch everything: identities, cars, backstory—"

"Backstory?"

"The story of where we come from, who we are. You need to learn your new identity. What Josie is like."

I sink down into the seat. I wonder what Eddie's doing now and whether I'll ever be allowed to contact him again. Right now he's probably playing soccer in the park. *He* doesn't have to learn how to be a girl. I can't believe I wanted him to see me in my new life—the thought of Eddie seeing me in this dress reminds me of how I felt after two turns on the Fear Factor fairground ride last summer.

Dad pops his head over the seat. "I'll show you the controls for the car before we get to work. For a start, let's get your seat adjusted." He leans forward and rests his hand on the dashboard for a moment. The dashboard glows under his fingers, enclosing them with neon green. As I watch, panels slide away to reveal six screens across the dashboard and hundreds of buttons.

"Whoa! This car's even better than the last one!"

"I know," Dad says, grinning. "Now, put your hand palm down next to you."

Dad flicks a few switches and presses a button marked READER. A moment later my seat's sliding forward. Dad's seat moves to the left. Now I'm almost level with Mom and Dad in the front.

Dan McGuire has a car seat like this in *Dan McGuire at Top Speed*. It pops up cans of soda and chocolate bars through the armrests. Maybe Mom and Dad can organize some customization later.

I search around for any buttons that might make something amazing happen—or get me out of here. "Is there an ejector seat?"

"Only in the movies, Joe." Dad fiddles with the dashboard panels. "Okay. Let's have a look at our new home."

On the middle screen a picture pops up of a detached house with a slate roof. There are flowers growing up around the front door like on those postcards you see on vacation.

It's not exactly the city apartment with mirror-black windows I've been imagining. I was thinking more of something on the twenty-sixth floor with an elevator that goes seventy miles per hour and walls that slide back to show three-hundred-inch televisions like in *Dan McGuire and the Techno Tyrant*.

"You see? It isn't all bad, Josie."

I groan and lean back. The gadgets are cool. The house looks okay. But I'll never get used to being a girl.

Dad brings up a screen of text. "Josephine Lily Marcus. Born the sixteenth of November."

"*Lily?*"

Dad ignores me. "No brothers or sisters, uncles or aunts. All grandparents deceased."

"What about Cousin Andrea?"

"Cousin Andrea's on a new mission," Mom says. "There is no Cousin Andrea."

"Josephine has an allergy to chlorine, which means she is never able to swim," Dad continues. "This has also added to a pre-existing fear of drowning, which prevents her from approaching any open water whatsoever."

"But I love swimming!"

"You can hardly go swimming now," Dad says. "Would give the game away a bit, wouldn't it?"

I picture myself in a bikini. It's enough to keep me from swimming for life.

I scowl at my reflection in the window. "Why don't you just put me down as loving makeup and be done with it."

"Do you mind?" Mom says. "What exactly do you think being a girl means?"

"It means I can't do anything I like. It means wearing stupid dresses and talking about make-up and . . . and . . . *pink stuff* all day long." I punch down the material of my dress, which is puffing up in the breeze from the air conditioning.

"I see we'll have to work on your attitude as well as your disguise," Mom says sharply.

Dad coughs and runs through the details of my place of birth, the story of my family, and the origin of my fear of water (a traumatic beach incident when I was three years old). I scratch at the edge of my wig as I try to concentrate. It looks like I'm going to have an itchy head for the next three to six months.

Three to six months!

"Josie?"

I drag a "yes" from my throat.

"Pay attention," Dad says.

Four hours later, I know my new life story back to front, and we're pulling up in front of the postcard house.

As Mom parks the car, a girl with spiky blond hair slams her way out of a house across the road from our new cottage. She's wearing tattered jeans, sneakers, and a light blue sweatshirt. The kind of clothes I used to wear all the time. The kind of clothes I'd kill for now. When she sees our car she stops and sits on the wall, staring over at us.

"Seems we have a neighbor," Dad says.

Mom turns to me. "Don't talk to her," she says. "You're not ready yet."

"Ready for what? Knowing how to ask her what her favorite shade of pink is?"

"Josie . . ." There's a warning note in Mom's voice.

"Okay, okay, I won't say anything."

As we get out of the car, Mom smiles and waves at the girl. "Hello!"

The girl half raises her hand in response. Then she gets down and walks up the hill at a very fast pace. Probably off to tell all her friends about the new funny looking girl who's moved to town.

The really ugly, funny looking girl.

Mom scoops a key out of her pocket and opens the front door, gesturing for us to follow. "Oh, Jed!" Mom exclaims. She's staring at the wood burner in the corner of the room. There's a wicker basket next to it piled high with chopped logs and kindling. The windows have deep sills and long curtains. There's a sofa against one of the walls. I slump down on it and stare at the wooden floor.

Mom comes over and rubs my shoulder. "It's really not that bad."

Yes. It really is.

Mom walks to the kitchen. A second later I hear a high-pitched beeping noise. Not the kind of beep a microwave makes when it's heated your

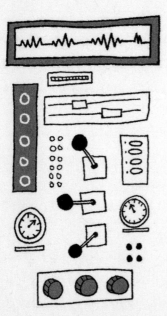

macaroni and cheese—a spy gadget beep. It's been less than twenty-four hours since Mom and Dad let me in on their secret and already I can tell the difference. So I've got the choice of staying on the sofa to prove to my parents that they've ruined my life or following Mom to find out what kind of spy gadgets are in the kitchen. I get up and follow Mom. I may as well make the most of the situation.

Mom is standing in front of a large pine pantry. The open door shows there are no shelves inside, just a black panel at the back. She presses some buttons on a silver keypad to the right of it and the panel slides open.

Mom jumps when she sees me. "You can't come in here."

"Why can't I—?"

"*Upstairs,*" Dad says. "It's not a game. This is serious."

I leave. When a Narnia pantry appears in the kitchen, you have to agree—it's serious.

Upstairs there are two bedrooms and a small bathroom. I go into the room with the single bed. The walls are strawberry-milkshake pink. The bedside table is pink. The comforter is pink with little red cherries. The lampshade is pink. It must be a rule—girls have to be surrounded by pink things *at all times*. I walk over to the window. The yard outside is perfect for soccer—wide, flat and bordered by tall hedges and trees. But who am I supposed to play with? If I were at home, I'd probably be in the park with Eddie, playing soccer and listening to him complain about his sister, Tilly. According to Eddie, girls are evil and only ever want to boss you around. And now I am one.

I sink down on the bed—also pink—and scratch my legs. The tights are making them itch almost as much as my head under the wig. So far being a girl seems to mean a lot of itching.

Mom and Dad appear. "Don't scratch so—" Mom says as there's a ripping sound and a hole appears in the right leg of my tights. She sighs. "Your first stocking run," she says. "Be more careful next time."

Yeah, because looking good is a real concern of mine.

"It'll all be better once you start school on Monday," Mom says, looping an arm around my shoulders.

"What?" That's the day after tomorrow! "I need time to adjust! This is a life-changing situation! I'm traumatized!"

Mom tilts her head to consider me. "You might be a little bit in shock, yes."

I let out a sigh of relief.

"But you're still going to school on Monday."

Chapter 5

In *Dan McGuire and the Coiling Cobra*, Dan McGuire is trained to wrestle snakes and crocodiles in the middle of the Nile River, bare-handed. I should be so lucky.

Dad starts my girl training on Sunday by making me walk across the room with books on my head.

"I thought they only do this *in* books."

"What's good enough for fiction is good enough for you."

So much for Dad feeling bad about making me be a girl.

Luckily, Mom arrives and saves me as Dad's debating whether or not I should learn how to curtsy. "What are you *doing*?"

"He's got to learn how to act the part, Zelia."

"He's not going to a finishing school, Jed! It's a perfectly ordinary elementary school."

"Yes, but to convince everyone, he's got to be as feminine as possible. A really girly girl." Dad reaches over and pinches my cheek. "He's got to be our little princess."

I just—I just can't speak.

"First of all, our son is not an actress or a dancer—it's a big enough challenge for him to learn how to put on a pair of tights without ripping them. I don't think we can expect miracles in his deportment. And second, how many elementary-school-aged girls have you seen acting like princesses?" Mom narrows her eyes at Dad—never a good sign.

"He's got to be girly enough that people believe he's a girl," Dad protests.

"Yes, but he won't do that by sticking out like

a sore thumb." Mom looks over at me. "Or a pink carnation—that dress has got to go. I'll find something a bit less . . . frilly."

"Thanks, Mom." I can't believe I'm grateful about the prospect of wearing a *less frilly dress.*

"But you've still got to do your best to be a convincing girl. That means no scratching, and no yanking at or ripping your tights."

Mom's brand of tights must be a *lot* more comfortable than mine.

Mom turns to Dad. "The cover story says that Josie's shy. That's what we should be concentrating on—if he can keep his mouth shut and stay in the background then he'll be fine."

"You mean I shouldn't have a personality?"

Mom doesn't pick up my tone or is ignoring it. "Right."

Dad's paper-thin cell phone warbles at him— he looks at it and then glances at Mom. "Got to check the screens."

By now I know that means he has to disappear into the secret spy room in the kitchen, the room I call Mission Control.

"Can I come?"

"No. You stay here and go over your cover with your mom. Don't want you slipping up on anything."

"When am I going to get to see what you *do*?"

Dad makes a zipping gesture across his mouth. "It's classified, I'm afraid."

"So, I'm stuck playing shy in a dress while you get to swan around doing *classified* stuff. Does that sound fair to you?"

Mom and Dad exchange a look.

"I suppose he should be a *little* familiar with what we do," Mom says.

"Okay. I'll show you the room and the gadgets," Dad says. "But not until tomorrow— after school. When you've proved you're taking this seriously."

It's not much, but it will have to do.

The next morning, Mom takes me to school. She's explained that our cover story is that we've relocated after both she and Dad found new jobs in the area. She's working part time as an interior designer for a chain of hotels, and Dad's in charge of checking security systems in stores and offices all over the region. It's a way they can keep moving to throw off the people trying to track them down and will make it easier to find out if they're still being followed. She reminds me for the billionth time that our enemies are looking for a family with a mom, dad, and son so any slip-up on my part could lead to us being discovered. No pressure, then.

"Once we're fairly sure we're not being watched, you can get the bus if you like," Mom says as we park outside the small brick building. "There's a service that goes from our village to this one." She glances over at me. "But maybe we should wait until you're confident about being able to keep your cover secure in all situations."

She'll be waiting a long time. I haven't even worked out how to keep my wig secure in all situations.

Walking into the school with Mom feels like there's a spotlight on me with a sign over my head that spells out FAKE GIRL. This morning I tried again to convince them that girls wear pants but even Mom agreed with Dad that I should stick with a skirt. Dad also made me wear an enormous pink smiley-faced butterfly clip in my wig. I'm doing my best to pretend it's not there. I wiggle my feet in the round-toed shoes, missing the soft give of my sneakers, and take a breath as the receptionist shows us into the principal's office.

"Hello, Josephine," Mrs. Harrison says, smiling. "I really hope you'll enjoy being with us at Bothen Hill School."

"Actually, we call her Josie," Mom says.

Like that's so much better.

I stare at the floor as Mom talks to Mrs. Harrison about me, explaining how shy I am, how I can't do any swimming because of my allergy to chlorine, how I prefer to keep quiet rather than join in activities. Josie sounds like the kind of person you'd want to stay a hundred miles away from.

I can't help thinking of Eddie—if I was at my old school now, we'd probably be whispering about the latest soccer match at the back of the class and getting scolded by Mr. Burnside. We'd be groaning about doing math and literacy and kicking each other under the table. I'd give anything to be back with Eddie right now, even if it meant a whole day of decimals.

Instead, I'm trying to stop myself from scratching the tops of my legs. They're itching like crazy but Mom says if I rip one more pair of tights I'll have to buy my own with my allowance money. And I really don't want to have to *pay* to be a girl.

"Well, I'm sure you need to be getting along so I'll take Josie down to Mr. Caulfield's class. I know everyone will give her a warm welcome." Mrs. Harrison gives me what I'm pretty sure is a pitying smile.

"Good luck, darling," Mom says. She waves and disappears out the door. There she goes, off to drive ninety miles an hour to her next spy mission while I have to face Complete Humiliation in front of strangers. Thanks, Mom.

My palms are clammy as I follow Mrs. Harrison down the hall to my new classroom. She knocks and then leads me into the room toward Mr. Caulfield at the front. He's got white hair and a beard and a round belly. I bet he gets asked to be Santa Claus at the school fair. I keep my eyes on him, avoiding looking at everyone else. My feet feel as if they've swollen to twice their size, and my skin is hot. I realize that I don't have to act shy—I *am* shy.

"Hello, Josie, welcome to the Crow class," Mr. Caulfield says as Mrs. Harrison gives me a reassuring pat on the arm and leaves. "Our classes are all named after birds—and since crows make a huge racket, it suits this class perfectly."

Everyone laughs as Mr. Caulfield leads me to a desk with an empty seat. "You can sit next to Sam." Sam turns out to be the girl we saw when we arrived at the new house. The one who saw me in the pink dress. She gives me a now-you-see-it-now-you-don't smile and turns away. I can't blame her. I wouldn't want to make friends with someone with my dress sense either.

My knees look really knobbly now that I'm sitting down. I cover them with my hands. I don't think it's normal for a girl to have knees like a bag of marbles.

Mr. Caulfield continues with the lesson. The work is all right—it's pretty much what I was doing at my old school—but I miss having Eddie to nudge in the ribs and laugh with. Eddie wasn't exactly the perfect friend. He complained a lot and you couldn't rely on him to stick up for you if you got in trouble. And if you ever did something stupid he'd laugh at you for days. But still, he was my friend and having a friend is better than being alone.

At least that's what I think until recess when I'm in the playground and every girl in the class comes up to me and fires questions at me. Why don't they want to do something *normal* like play a game of soccer instead of standing around *chatting*?

"Do you like it here?"

"What was your old school like?"

"Why did you move?"

"Where do you live?"

"Where did you get your hair clip?"

I keep my answers short but I'm starting to panic. I'm supposed to stay in the background! I'm supposed to keep my wig straight and stay quiet! Luckily, my one-word answers make them lose interest in me and after a while I'm left by the side of the playground, watching people talk and play games.

I knew having spy parents would turn my life upside down, but I didn't think it would mean I'd be lonely.

I catch sight of Sam. She's playing soccer. She tries to take a shot at the goal but she's tackled and the ball shoots over toward me. Automatically, I run forward and trap the ball with my foot. She looks a bit surprised but she gestures toward the goal. I take the shot, and it goes in. Kicking the ball is the first natural thing I've done in days.

Sam whistles. "Good goal."

I can't stop myself grinning at her. "Thanks."

Then I remember—Josie's not supposed to be sporty. I have to get out of here before I do anything else to mess up my cover.

I hurry back to our wing and down the hall to the bathrooms. I have my hand on the door and I'm about to push through to the other side when a boy from my class stops and laughs.

"Where are you going?"

"What?"

I look up at the sign on the door I'd been about to go through—to the boys' bathroom.

Well done, Josie. Two mistakes in less than a minute. I'm starting to understand how hard keeping up this cover is going to be.

"I wasn't going *in*, I just wanted to get something off my shoe," I tell him. I lift up my foot, still leaning against the door, and brush something imaginary from it.

The boy keeps laughing. Which makes me want to do something I'm pretty sure isn't on Dad's list of Acceptable Girly Girl Behavior.

"Leave her alone, Paul. She's only new." Another boy is walking up to us.

Laughing Boy shrugs. He jams his hands in his pockets and wanders off.

"Ignore him," says the boy. "He's being stupid."

"Thanks."

"My name's Noah."

"Okay. I'm Joe . . . sie."

"Yeah. Okay. Well, see you." Noah walks off.

I sigh. When I was at my old school, I was never interested in talking to the girls, either.

I go into the girls' bathroom. Luckily there's no one there. I lock myself into one of the stalls. Maybe I can stay in here every recess. Mom and Dad can come up with a reason for me having to shut myself away—some sort of illness or a phobia. I could be frightened of any room that doesn't have a toilet in it.

I hear the door swing open, and then the sound of a girl's voice, and then another and another. In seconds it sounds like every single girl from the school has come in.

If I could flush myself down the toilet to get out of here, I would.

I'll have to brave it. Maybe I can sneak out and no one will notice. I open the stall door and inch toward the door.

A soccer crowd of girls swivels round.

"There you are, Josie!" says one of the girls from the playground. "We were worried about you."

"It must be hard starting a new school," says another.

"No . . . I'm fine." I give a tiny smile and take another step toward the door.

Sam is with them. "You live across the street from me, don't you?"

"Yeah."

"So, you like soccer?"

I'm about to say no—I'm not supposed to like activities. "Remember, you're too shy to join in things," Dad told me this morning. But Sam plays soccer. Sam might even like to talk about soccer. Can it really be that dangerous to be honest just once?

"Yeah, I love it."

"Good." She studies me. "That was a nice goal in the playground. Maybe you can try out for the girls' team."

"I don't know." I can't tell her Mom and Dad are worried enough about the risk of me being discovered in gym class. I can't see them agreeing for me to do something sporty when I don't have to. Plus, it goes against the whole not-joining-in identity Josie's supposed to have. I'm not even allowed to ask anyone over to our house. But the thought of being able to play, even on a girls' team, is hard to resist.

"You really should," Sam says. "Jess has dropped out for the semester because she broke her leg. We could use someone who knows what they're doing."

"Hey," says a girl with dark hair tied back in a ponytail. "You're not the only good player, you know."

"I know. But we still need someone else on the team." Sam turns to me. "So, will you come to practice after school tomorrow?"

She looks so sure I'll agree that I find myself nodding.

Keeping out of things is harder than it sounds.

Chapter 6

"I don't know if you playing soccer is such a great idea," Dad says when I tell Mom and Dad about Sam's invite.

"It's a *girls'* team. It's not like I'll be out of disguise."

"But there are so many ways you could be discovered. What about when you get changed? What if your wig falls off in a match?"

"I've got to handle all that for gym anyway. I'll pretend to be shy. I'll get changed in the bathroom. And Mom bought me a headband and extra barrettes to help keep my wig on."

"I don't know." Dad rubs his chin where his beard used to be.

"I've had to move away from home and all my friends. I have to dress up like a girl! You could at least let me join the school soccer team!"

Mom and Dad look at each other. Then I see Mom give an almost invisible shrug that means only one thing—victory.

"You'll have to be really, really careful," Dad tells me.

"I will!"

Dad's about to say something else when they get one of those phone beeps that means they have to disappear into Mission Control.

"I thought you were showing me the gadgets today?" I remind him.

Dad sighs. "Yeah. But the job we're doing right now . . . well, it's tricky."

Mom fishes in her purse and hands me a few dollars. "Why don't you run down to the shop at the corner? Buy yourself some chocolate. We should be done by the time you're back."

"You're just trying to get rid of me," I say, but I take the money.

I nearly don't go to the shop. Mom hasn't had time to buy some other dresses yet so out of school I'm still stuck in the pink *thing* that Dad bought. But I decide I need chocolate more than dignity.

The woman behind the counter smiles at me when I come up. "Hello, princess. What a pretty dress!"

Princess?! I drop my chocolate bar on the counter and hand her my money, restraining myself from throwing it at her.

"You're new around here, aren't you, sweetie?"

Sweetie?! "We just moved." My jaw's clenched so tight my teeth might crack.

"Here, you can have them as a welcome present," she says, giving back my money and then pushing the chocolate over to me with a smile.

"Thanks," I say, snatching up the chocolate from the counter. *Princess* and *sweetie!* It's not even worth free chocolate.

I push my way out of the shop and slump down on the wall. The chocolate lasts about a second. I pull out my phone and play seven games of Mega Tank in a row to calm myself down, but I can't even get past level one. If Eddie were here he'd be laughing like crazy. I've got disguise trauma!

"Mega Tank?" The voice makes me jump.

It's Sam. Uh oh. I stand up. Sam holds out her hand and I realize she wants to look at the phone. I give it to her, wishing I could think of a reason not to.

She swipes it to life, tapping at it expertly. "Mega Tank, Dark Destroyer, Sonic Slicer . . . these are kind of boys' games, aren't they?"

"My dad put them on."

"Doesn't he have his own phone?"

"He ran over it with his car." Quick thinking isn't clever thinking. Why can't I keep my mouth shut?

"But there aren't any other games on here. You must like them, too."

My skin goes cold. But Dad's always said attack is the best line of defense. "Why can't girls play those games?"

"Of course they can. It's just, with a phone like this—you know, really pink—and what you wear being so . . . so . . ."

We both look at my dress. It's hard not to see her point.

"But then you like soccer . . ." She shrugs. "It's a bit strange, that's all."

My stomach's doing flips—I keep hearing Dad in my head saying, "This is serious."

I reach out and take the phone back. "*You* like it, too."

"Yeah, but—"

"I'd better get back." I've got to get out of here before I do something else that alerts her to the fact I am *not a normal girl.*

"Don't forget soccer tomorrow!" she calls after me as I set off for home.

As if. It's forgetting how to keep my cover in place that's the problem.

At home, Dad's finally ready to show me some of their gadgets.

"All right, look. I'm going to trust you."

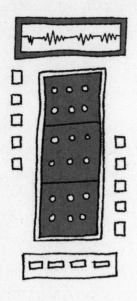

We're standing in front of the panel to Mission Control. He presses the code into the steel pad. I crane my neck so that I can memorize it. I figure it's good practice. Who knows, I might go into the spy business myself someday. Mr. Burnside once said that kids often go into the same field as their parents. Back when Dad was supposed to be in politics and Mom was in computers, I wasn't that impressed. But growing up to be James Bond would be awesome. Especially in pants.

The black panel at the back of the cupboard slides open. Dad gestures me in. "Quickly." The panel swishes shut behind us.

We've walked into a large room where every wall is covered with glowing blue screens. It's like the flight deck of a space ship. There are panels covered with buttons and receivers set into the wall that look like a cross between a telephone and a walkie-talkie. There are slots for USB drives as well as for CDs and DVDs. Shelves on the right-hand side are crammed with techy looking gear. It's a sweet shop of spy gadgets—and it's my mom and dad's office! Car chases are one thing but this room makes me realize that Mom and Dad are *real* spies.

"Take a seat." Dad points at one of the two swivel chairs, and I sit down as he takes his position in front of the shelves. "So. First you have your classic spy stationery," he says. "Cameras in pens, erasers, rulers, staplers." He holds up a pencil sharpener. "You can hide a camera in almost anything these days."

I take one of the rulers and examine it, seeing how the design incorporates a tiny eye and, along the edge, a miniature button.

"Same goes for recording devices." Dad shuffles through stuff on the next shelf and picks up some headphones. "Mic in one ear and operating buttons in the other. 'Course, some are

a bit more imaginative." He roots around and holds up a bottle of Wite-Out. "Unscrew the cap a little and it starts recording; screw it back down and it stops."

"That's amazing!" I could have had so much fun with that with Mr. Burnside.

Dad pulls out a small black box. "And this is one of my favorites."

"What is it?"

"It's a disrupter."

"A what?"

"A disrupter. Imagine you're after something, but there's a crowd around and you don't want witnesses. This creates a disruption for you wherever you set it, to distract attention from whatever you need to do."

I wish Eddie and I had been able to get our hands on a disrupter. We could have *definitely* used it. "What kind of disruption?"

"Oh, you can choose from a range. A little fire—controlled, of course—or a series of bangs that might be mistaken for gunshots or a car misfiring. Or fireworks—really small ones. Or an alarm—that kind of thing." Dad pats it affectionately before putting it back.

I can't help staring as he rummages around on another shelf. I can't believe this gadget-wielding spy is my dad. He once killed our lawn mower by pouring oil in the gas tank and now he knows how to operate miniature recording devices?

Dad smiles as if he's read my mind before continuing with his demonstration. "Then we have all the voice-activated recording equipment embedded in coins, pens, sunglasses . . . and these are always useful, of course." He holds up a handful of silver and gold watches.

"What, for when you're pretending to be selling Rolex knock-offs?"

"No. These all have double and triple functions—some are phones, some are recorders, some are detonators—"

"*Detonators?*"

Dad coughs. "Yeah, I'll tell you about that another time." He pulls out a little book. "This is excellent."

"A pocket calendar?"

"Look." Dad flips the pages until he gets to the end. Then, the whole book turns inside out and I can see a miniature keyboard and screen. "Miniature laptop with untraceable Internet access. Fantastic for hacking." He picks up a thin, round silver case.

"What's that?"

"Your mom uses this all the time. Looks like a compact mirror—but it's actually a video-phone and camera. You press the buttons here to switch between the functions."

He takes out more stuff as I try to imagine Mom and Dad in action with it all, uncovering enemy secrets. It gives me an excited shivery feeling, like sitting in a dark movie theater the moment before a film starts. I'm having to get to know my mom and dad all over again.

Dad goes on. "Motion detector alarm clock, bugging devices in an adaptor, in a clothes hanger, in an egg timer, a paper clip, a packet of sugar. Here's a bionic ear for listening in to conversations up to a mile away. Always useful, that one. And here's another one of my favorites— Internet dental floss."

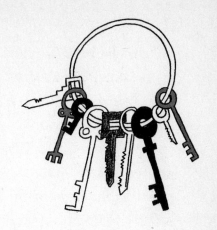

"What?" *Internet dental floss*? Even brushing my teeth could become a scene from a spy film!

Dad taps the box. "Flip open the top and instead of dental floss you have a little wi-fi antennae. Lovely piece of equipment."

"And these keys?" I point to a bunch on the desk in front of me.

"They open things. *Anything*, in fact." He picks up the keys and gives them a fond look. "They can get you into any lock you want."

"*Any* lock?" I hold out my hand and Dad lobs them over.

"Anything at all. If there's a lock on it, there's a key there to fit it."

"And how about this?" Dad pulls a long, thin steel cable from the pile. He waves it at me. "This is a version of what we used the other night. It latches onto a roof or window or whatever so you can climb out of sticky situations. It's military-grade steel."

I wonder how many times Dad's used it. It's weird to think of Mom and Dad as action heroes. Though considering what they've been making me do, "heroes" might be a bit of an exaggeration.

Dad shows me how the pen cameras work and how they can be inserted into slots in the wall to transfer or print the digital images, and where recordings can be transferred onto memory sticks. As he's tapping screens and flicking buttons, I get an image of him as he used to be—spilling coffee in the car and making really bad Dad jokes. Now he's showing me the tricks of the spy trade.

Grown-ups go on about how kids change so fast but no one ever talks about when *they* change overnight.

Dad pulls out a black sack. "And this is essential."

"What's in it?"

"Different characters." He puts his hand in the sack and pulls out a pair of thick-rimmed glasses and pops them on his nose. Then he reaches back in and takes out a black hat, which he pulls down low over his forehead. Once more into the bag and this time it's a set of sideburns, which he sticks to his cheeks. He faces me. "You see? I've become someone else."

"No. You're Dad with a hat, glasses, and bad facial hair." I grin at him. The dad from our old life liked dressing up, too. Maybe he hasn't changed as much as I thought. "Everyone would know it's you if they looked hard enough," I tell him.

"That's the point. Most people *don't* look hard enough. Most people only see what they're looking for—if you give them something different, they simply won't recognize it."

"No, sorry, don't know what you're talking about."

"Look. Picture a friend in your mind."

Weirdly, instead of Eddie, I think of Sam. I picture her short, spiky blond hair and her sharp right foot on the ball. "Okay. Now what?"

"If you look for him in the street you know what you'll be looking for, right?"

"Well, yeah . . ."

"But if someone who's a lot taller than him with a different hair color walks by, will you think it's him?"

"No, course not."

"But it *could* be. Your friend could dye his hair, put on some heeled shoes, and you wouldn't even glance at him because he *wouldn't be what you were expecting to see.*"

This does explain why I haven't been immediately found out as a Not Very Believable Girl. And maybe it's also why I never suspected my parents weren't what they said they were for all those years. I think of how many secrets they've kept from me and how much I have left to find out.

"All you have to remember is that people don't notice half as much as you think. Unless they're a spy, of course." Dad smiles and picks up a bag from the bottom shelf. "What do you think of this?" Dad digs into the bag and then throws a soccer ball at me.

I catch it and weigh it in my hands. It's amazing quality—the kind of ball that professionals play with—heavy and solid. "It's a beauty."

"It's yours. Hope it brings you luck when you try out for the team."

"Thanks!" There's a seam in one side that's thicker than the rest. I bring it close to my face to examine it.

"Keep talking," Dad tells me, and reaches out to touch the side of the ball.

"I don't understand. Isn't it a normal soccer ball?"

"That's enough."

Dad presses the ball again, and my voice comes out. "I don't understand. Isn't it a normal soccer ball?"

"It's a recorder?"

"Yeah. But it's also a high-class bit of soccer equipment—the sound equipment is encased in steel so you can whack the ball as hard as you like without worrying about damaging the recorder. I

wanted to give you something to make up for all this stuff going on. And maybe it will come in useful sometime."

"Uh . . . and why would a recording soccer ball be useful?"

"Trust me. You never know." Dad shows me where the almost invisible buttons are, just inside the seam. "Simple to use, too. Press once to record, press again to stop, press the other button to play it back."

It really *is* an awesome soccer ball. "Thanks, Dad."

"No problem. I know it's hard on you, all this."

Tell me about it. I don't just deserve a soccer ball, I deserve a medal.

Chapter 7

The next morning, Mom pulls up in front of the school without turning off the engine. She checks her rearview mirror, then reaches over me to pop open the glove compartment. Inside, a slim steel box with a row of tiny green lights is whirring softly. Mom glances at it, then clicks the compartment shut.

"What does that do?" I ask her.

She smiles as she pulls my bag from the back seat and hands it to me. "Satellite technology. It tracks people and cars in the surrounding area and analyzes patterns of movement so we can pick up on any unusual behavior."

"You mean, like people following us."

"Exactly. You have to be on your guard—especially when you're following your normal routines. That's when you're most at risk. Now, off you go."

I look at the clock on the dashboard. "Attendance is not for ten minutes."

"So?"

"So that's ten extra minutes for me to risk blowing my cover." After my conversation with Sam yesterday, I figure I should cut down the amount of time I have to talk to anyone.

"I've got things to do," Mom says. "Besides, you need to become confident with your new identity." She pats my knee. "Don't worry, it'll get easier."

Grown-ups always say this. I think they forget that the amount of time needed for something to get easier is the time it takes for you to become so ancient you've forgotten how hard things can be.

"Now, do you have the headband and barrettes to keep your wig on during soccer?"

"Yes."

"Excellent. Good luck, sweetheart. We'll see you later."

I get out of the car and trudge toward the school. I'm pretty sure I know what prisoners feel like when they go to jail.

"Hey, Josie!" A girl from my class rushes up to me as I push through the gate. "I'm Melissa, I sit behind you."

"Hi." I flash her my best "shy smile" and tip my head so that my wig hair falls across my face. I have to admit, long hair does have its uses.

"A few of us are meeting in the hall at lunch break. Why don't you come, too?"

"Um . . ." Stress freezes my brain. I know I need to find a reason not to say yes. I know the same way birds sense a cat creeping up behind them in the garden.

"You must be really lonely after leaving your old school. Did you have lots of friends there?"

I keep my head down and mutter, "Don't know. Not really."

"You've got to come then. Everyone's really nice. We're doing something really good. You'll love it." Melissa waves at someone across the playground. "I'll come and find you after lunch."

She's off before I can think of an excuse, or can break one of my own legs. I'll have to talk to Mom and Dad. I don't think they know what girls are like about getting you to join in with things. I remember Eddie saying that when his sister Tilly was younger, she held people hostage in her room and forced them to have tea with her teddy bears. I wish I could tell him that I understand what he was talking about now.

Mr. Caulfield is halfway through the morning language arts lesson on metaphors and similes (I hate being a girl like a soccer player hates an own goal) when Mrs. Harrison pops her head around the door.

"Sorry to disturb you," she says. "I just wanted to give you those files you asked for."

Mr. Caulfield hurries over and takes a large yellow folder from her. He looks as if she's told him he's won the lottery. "I'm so grateful to you for offering to do this," Mrs. Harrison says. "We're having a nightmare finding a good accountant."

Mr. Caulfield smiles. "It's no trouble. I want to do as much as I can for the school before I retire."

For someone who's taken on extra work, Mr. Caulfield looks really happy about it. But maybe he's not thinking about the work, maybe he's thinking about his retirement. I really hope by the time Mr. Caulfield leaves, I'll be long gone and back to being myself again and away from all these girls. Three to six months, Dad said.  And to use another simile, maybe, like a good prisoner, I might even get out early for good behavior. The thought makes me smile.

I eat my sandwich quickly and slip out of the side door into the playground, planning to head for the bathroom again. This time I just won't come out of the stall. But as I'm heading toward our wing, a hand grabs my elbow.

"There you are!" Melissa tugs at me. "Come on, it's this way." She keeps her hand tight on my arm the whole way to the hall—like a hooked fish, I have absolutely no chance of escaping.

There are two other girls waiting for us. One is fiddling with an iPod dock and the other one is standing in a pose like she's on a magazine cover.

"That's Nerida and Suzy," says Melissa. The girls wave at me.

"We're doing a dance routine for the end of the semester Achievers' Assembly," Melissa says. "You can learn it with us."

"A dance?" My chest tightens, and my breath catches in my throat.

Melissa doesn't notice that I'm becoming *very sick*. "Don't worry, it's really easy. Watch us first, and then you can join in."

Join in? I'm more likely to pass out!

The girl named Nerida presses PLAY and some boy-band song blasts out. The three girls wiggle around the room like eels, waving their arms in the air and grinning as if they've just been given tickets to the Stanley Cup final.

I take a step backward toward the door, staring in horror as they put their hands on their hips and circle them around and around. How do they even *do* that? I'm not convinced that girls are completely human.

Nerida and Suzy waggle their fingers as if they're petting an invisible cat—lots of invisible cats. Melissa puts her hands behind her back and sways from side to side. Maybe she's got an itch in a hard-to-reach place. When they see me staring they erupt into giggles. I have no idea what they think is so funny but they're hurting my ears.

Melissa kind of shimmies over to me and grabs my hand. "Come on, Josie, it's easy!" She pulls me across the floor.

"NOOOO!"

Melissa drops my hand. "What's the matter?"

They stare at me as the song comes to an end.

"I . . . um . . . I have a bruise. Where you touched me." I pull my sleeve down.

"Oh, sorry."

Maybe if I wish really, really hard, the ground will open up and they will VANISH.

Luckily, the bell rings before I can do anything else to get myself in trouble.

"Don't worry," Melissa says, "there's lots of time to learn the dance."

"I don't think I can. I've got, um, problems with my arches."

"Oh." Melissa sounds disappointed. She wouldn't be if she could see me dance.

In the playground, Sam catches up with me as I'm walking back. "I saw you come out with Melissa and her gang. So, you like dancing?"

Before I can stop myself, the words burst out, "I hate it!"

She looks a bit surprised. "Oh. Well, soccer practice is only a few hours away. You'll enjoy that."

"Yeah." I decide to keep my head down for

the afternoon. I've got to learn how to keep my mouth shut.

My soccer outfit isn't perfect—it's *light-years* away from perfect. The tracksuit bottoms are baggy and have way too many flowers on them. But at least it isn't a dress. As soon as the bell rings, I lock myself in the bathroom to get changed and make sure my headband and barrettes are securely in place. I don't need any more disguise slip-ups today. I drop my gym bag at the edge of the playground and bounce the soccer ball Dad gave me as I walk toward Sam and the others. I almost—*almost*—feel all right.

"Nice ball," Sam says, "but we're only supposed to use the school balls." Then Sam takes the ball from me and grins. "Mr. Caulfield is still getting the cones for practice, though, so let's give it a quick test." She flicks the ball up onto her chest then lets it drop to the ground, resting her right foot on top of it. "Ready?"

I fix my eyes on the ball. "Go."

Sam heads toward the net with a clean kick. I hold back a bit, not wanting to embarrass her right away.

She scores a perfect goal.

Fluke.

Sam retrieves the ball and, when I try to tackle her, easily sidesteps me.

Another goal.

Another fluke.

Next time, I go after her the same way I'd have gone after Eddie. I manage to get the ball from her for a second before Sam reclaims it.

Another goal.

What is *going on*?!

Mr. Caulfield appears and blows a whistle. Sam passes me the ball and we walk towards him.

"Good shots," I tell her, trying not to sound shocked.

"Good tackling."

For a second I think she's making fun of me, the way Eddie would have done, and then I realize she's serious. "Thanks."

"Hello, Josie, I'm glad you've decided to join us." Mr. Caulfield points at my ball. "But didn't anyone tell you you're only allowed to use school equipment?"

"Sorry, I just really wanted to try it out."

"That's all right. But I'm afraid I'll have to confiscate it until practice is over." He holds his hands out and I reluctantly pass it over. "I just have to make a quick call so you all go ahead and get yourselves warmed up."

By the time we've done a few stretches and laps around the field, Mr. Caulfield's back and proper play gets underway. About halfway through the practice I realize that I'm getting a better game as Josie than I ever did as Joe. I've had more time on the ball than any match I've ever played—the girls are great about passing—and my side wins! It's awesome! At the end, Mr. Caulfield gives me my ball back and Sam and I talk soccer while we wait to be picked up at the gate.

I'm planning to tell Mom all about it, but as soon as I get in the car she puts her finger to her lips. "Sorry, sweetheart. I'm waiting for a call from HQ—can we chat later?"

"Oh, okay." I guess it's natural that in our new life, spy stuff comes first and my stuff comes second, but that doesn't mean it's easy.

Mom pats my hand and pulls out onto the road. "It's such a relief that we've been able to tell you the truth about what we do. It's good to know you understand we can't always give you as much attention as before."

Then Mom's hands-free phone rings and she's talking in code about mission this and mission that while I stare out of the window. When I imagined living the life of Dan McGuire, this isn't exactly what I had in mind.

When we get home, Dad tells me my dinner is on a plate in the fridge and to microwave it when I'm hungry. Then he and Mom disappear into Mission Control.

You'd think having spies for parents would be non-stop excitement. You'd think I'd be learning about code-breaking and computer hacking and catching villains.

You'd be wrong.

Up in my room, I'm practicing spinning the soccer ball on my finger when I touch the PLAY switch by mistake. Mr. Caulfield's voice is loud and clear. "Now that we've got the files, you can transfer the funds. I'll let you know when the grant money comes into the school and then you can put that into my account as well."

There's a pause as a distant, muffled voice says something. Then it's back to Mr. Caulfield. "Look, by the time Mrs. Harrison realizes, I'll have taken my early retirement and be long gone. You do your part and I'll do mine. Okay?"

A phone clatters onto a receiver and that's it—there's nothing else on the recording.

Mr. Caulfield must have activated the recording device when he took the ball into school during soccer practice. But why was he having a conversation about putting school money into his own bank account? I suppose it must be something to do with him doing that accounting work for Mrs. Harrison. He's not exactly the criminal type. People who look like Santa Claus don't commit crimes.

But the recording gives me an idea—if Mom and Dad won't train me to be a spy, maybe I can train myself. And I think I've found a perfect first practice case.

Chapter 8

Family breakfasts just aren't the same these days. Dad used to make oatmeal or hard-boiled eggs, Mom would make tea and toast, and we'd all sit around quietly, maybe with them asking me a couple of questions about school and me grunting into my bowl until they told me to hurry up or I'd be late. Like a normal family.

Not any more.

Now Mom or Dad rush around garbling code words, or one of them disappears off into Mission

Control or sits hunched over a laptop, peering at the screen, or punches numbers into their phone, or goes off in the car on some secret errand. Or sometimes Mom is in a corner of the room talking into her spy compact. And now that I take the bus with Sam, I don't even see them on the way to and from school. It's as if telling me the truth has given them a License to Ignore their son. But at least I can continue with my investigation in peace.

While I eat breakfast I decide on a plan. My soccer ball recording is going to be the basis for my first spy mission. It doesn't matter if it turns out that Mr. Caulfield isn't doing anything wrong as long as I learn how to be a good spy. Then maybe I can convince Mom and Dad to let me help them on one of their missions—or at least give me real training.

First of all I need to borrow some of Mom and Dad's equipment. When Dad runs upstairs for his shower and Mom's gone off for her latest appointment, I punch the code into the pad and slip inside Mission Control. I grab a selection of spy gear and I'm out again in seconds. I have just enough time to pile it all in my backpack before having to meet Sam at the bus stop.

We talk about soccer all the way. Sam even likes Santos! When I'm talking to her, I almost forget who I am—or who I'm supposed to be.

But when I see Melissa in the playground, it all comes back with a sinking-stomach rush.

"Hi, Josie! Here." She hands me an envelope and smiles. "My birthday party's tomorrow after school. I'd really like you to come."

"Um, thanks." She's wearing a barrette with a pink butterfly on it that's a lot like mine so I guess she's forgiven me for not joining in the dancing. I can take being friends with Sam—she's normal! She likes soccer! But Melissa looks like the kind of girly girl Dad wants me to be. It's a bit too close for comfort.

I follow Sam into our wing and we hang up our coats. Dad's insisted I wear the one he bought— it's dark pink with sequins on the collar. I sigh as I watch Sam put her dark blue jacket on the hook.

"So, are you going?" Sam nods at the envelope from Melissa.

"Uh, maybe." No chance. I just need to come up with an excuse. Mom and Dad said I should keep to myself so they'll be happy for me not to go. I'll be spared Melissa and her balloon animals—or whatever she's having at her party.

I concentrate on keeping an eye on Mr. Caulfield during literacy and math. He keeps running out to get things he's forgotten—paper, Wite-Out, a new pad of paper. It's probably because he's getting old and losing his memory, but I have to think with a spy brain—he *could* be making more phone calls. The only way to find out is to plant some recording equipment on him.

I've just got to figure out how.

After recess, we go to the community pool for swimming. I sit next to Sam on the bus and she tells me how she learned to swim when her mom took her to Greece.

"It was so warm and there were fish everywhere. It was like swimming in an aquarium."

"You're lucky," I tell her. "I learned in a pool down the road from where we used to live. Once

I saw an old man blow his nose in the shallow end and my mom still wouldn't let me get out!"

Sam laughs. Then she frowns—just as I realize what I've said. "But I thought Mr. Caulfield said you were allergic to chlorine. Isn't that why you're not swimming today?"

Mom and Dad should have sewn my mouth shut.

"Yeah, but . . . the pool I was talking about didn't have any chlorine in it. It was a special pool."

"But you told me you're afraid of water as well."

"It was ages ago," I say quickly. "Before I was afraid. Or allergic."

"Oh." Sam has *I'm not sure I believe you* written all over her face. I can see she's working up to another question and decide to get in there first.

"When's Mr. Caulfield retiring?"

"Next summer. I think that's what my mom said. We'll have Mr. Sentance in September."

"Oh, right, of course. I heard him talking about it, that's all." I know from Dan McGuire how important it is to collect background information on your subject. I guess next summer is what Mr. Caulfield meant by early retirement.

When we walk into the pool, Mr. Caulfield sends everyone off to get changed. I wait, wondering where to go and wishing I could follow the rest of the boys. Just the smell of chlorine makes me want to do a cannonball into the water.

"Go through the changing rooms, Josie, and then you can sit and read on the bleachers on the other side."

Walk through the girls' changing rooms? Is he joking? "Isn't there another way?"

Mr. Caulfield looks surprised.

"I don't think so. Anyway, I'd prefer you to stick with the other girls, okay?"

No. It's not okay at all.

I take a deep breath and keep my eyes down— but that doesn't stop me hearing things.

"My bra straps are killing me," Nerida says.

I speed up but because I've got my eyes on the floor I nearly walk right into Melissa.

"Do you wear a bra, Josie?"

"YOU HAVE GOT TO BE JOKING!"

Everyone stares at me.

Mom and Dad might be spies, but I don't think they have a clue how stressful this undercover stuff is.

Being on the bleachers during the swimming lesson makes me think of our old life. I used to love swimming. Eddie liked playing this game called submarines. One person was the submarine and one person was the missile. You took turns being the missile and trying to sink the submarine. The only problem was that Eddie was a lot bigger than me and so he was a lot better at being the missile. By the end of the game, I'd be half drowned. But most of the time swimming was fun, though if it was with school we always ended up getting shouted at by Mr. Burnside. Mr. Burnside wasn't a fan of submarines.

I've brought my favorite Dan McGuire book, *Dan McGuire and the Code-Cracker*, but it's hard to concentrate when everyone else is splashing around and laughing. Then Mr. Caulfield sits a couple of rows in front of me. I forget all about the swimming lesson and the book because Mr. Caulfield has his cell phone in his hand. This is my chance to do a secret recording!

I inch my leg over the seat in front of me so that I can drop into the row directly behind him. He doesn't notice me. He's already talking by the time I'm in earshot. I click on my recording pen and hold it out as far as I can. His conversation might turn out to be boring but at least I'll be getting some practice in.

"I've had an excellent idea of how to add to our takings . . . a little charity work project. It will mean we have to move quickly—but I think it could improve both our bank balances. There's only so much money to be gained from the local council's grants, after all."

There's a pause as Mr. Caulfield listens.

"Mark, Mark, you worry too much. You forget that I've been at Bothen Hill School for fifteen years—why would anyone suspect me? I'm just making sure my bank balance will be big enough for me to live on when I retire."

Not so boring after all.

The community pool's swimming instructor blows a whistle and everyone swims back to the end of the pool. I quickly pull out my book and bury myself in the pages as Mr. Caulfield says goodbye and pockets his cell phone.

"Josie!"

I pretend to be lost in my book and only react after a second. "Oh, hello, Mr. Caulfield."

"I didn't see you there." Mr. Caulfield's smile doesn't quite reach his eyes.

"I came back from the bathroom and then got into my book, sir."

"You like to underline your favorite parts, don't you?" Mr. Caulfield nods at the recording pen still in my hand.

"Yeah."

I must sound convincing. Mr. Caulfield relaxes. "Well, I'm glad you found a way to pass the time, Josie, well done."

I've definitely found a way to pass the time. Spying on Mr. Caulfield looks as if it might prove to be a real mission after all.

Chapter 9

Mom picks up a piece of microfilm with some tweezers and carefully puts it on the top right-hand corner of an envelope. Then she peels off a stamp and sticks it down on top of the film. I'm getting used to this kind of thing now. It's almost like watching her doing the ironing. Mom hands the envelope over to Dad and then looks at me. "Well, I think you should go."

"What? You said I should keep in the background! You said I shouldn't join in things!"

"Yes, but then you decided to join the soccer team," says Mom. "So that's changed your cover story already, hasn't it?"

"And you say this Melissa is 'girly' so I think it's an excellent idea for you to be friends with her. It will make you more believable." Dad addresses the envelope with his left hand, which turns his handwriting into an almost illegible scrawl.

"No, it will make me more miserable."

"It's a birthday party. What's not to like?" Mom looks at my face. "Don't answer that."

After school, Melissa's mom picks up everyone who's going to the party. On the way to Melissa's house, I pretend to laugh whenever they do, even though I don't really understand what they're laughing about. Eddie's mom had a friend from France who used to come and stay with them. They'd speak French really fast and when I was over at Eddie's, I'd feel really embarrassed to hear them, as if I should know what they were saying.

I feel the same way now—and they're talking English!

We arrive at Melissa's house and go into the living room. "Surprise!" Melissa throws out her arms. "Pamper party!"

I have no idea what a pamper party is but it takes about three seconds to guess. Every surface is covered with make-up, hairbrushes, sparkly hair clips, and some steel roddy-type things with plugs. It's detention with torture.

"Who's up for the first makeover?"

I can't help it. I make a squeaking sound.

"Are you all right, Josie?"

"Can I have a drink of water?"

"Of course, help yourself." Melissa's mom smiles at me. "I'm so looking forward to doing your hair, Josie, it's so pretty."

You're not laying a finger on me, Lady. Sam follows me into the kitchen. "Are you okay?"

I gulp down a glass of water. And then another one. And then another one. Problem solved—I'll stay in the bathroom for the entire party!

"Yeah, sure," I say. I just need to come up with a reason why no one can touch my face or my head.

I go back into the living room and up to Melissa's mom. She's busy putting dark blue stuff on Nerida's eyelids with a plastic stick.

"How do I look?" Nerida grins up at me.

"Nice." If you like pandas.

"I'll be able to do you in a minute, Josie," Melissa's mom says.

"That's okay. Actually, I'm a bit allergic, so I'll just watch."

"Oh, dear—I'm sorry. But even if you can't have makeup on, I can still give you a nice hair-do."

"No!"

Melissa's mom holds her stick in mid-air and looks at me.

"I mean, my head is really sensitive."

Sam snorts.

"I see." Melissa's mom shoots a look at Melissa. You can see she's thinking, *Who is this weird girl?*

"I know!" Melissa grabs a nail file and waves it at me like a knife. "Mom can do your nails!"

"Oh, no, I—"

"Come on, Josie, it'll be great!"

Melissa drags me over to the sofa and pushes me down so that I'm sitting in front of her mom. Melissa's mom finishes off Nerida's face by smearing her lips in bright pink goo and then leans over and grabs one of my hands. "You're going to love this."

I'm really not.

She files my nails into points like a cat. Great, now I have claws. Then she paints them with purple, foul-smelling glossy paint. Just when I think the agony is over, she decides to stick little sparkly stickers, all different shades of pink, on each nail. My hands have been turned into finger puppets!

"There. Isn't that lovely?" Melissa's mom asks proudly.

Melissa, Nerida, and Suzy coo over my hands like they're kittens.

I have to get out of here.

"I'm just going to get some more water," I say, getting up from the sofa and backing towards the kitchen.

"I'll come, too," Sam says. "I'm not excited about getting a makeover."

Wait, it's that easy? Why didn't I say that?

"Well, there are some craft-making things in the kitchen," Melissa's mom says. "I was planning on that for later, but you could start now if you don't want to have your face and hair done."

"Great!" I sound extra enthusiastic to balance things out.

We find blank cards, pens, glue, and about a thousand pots of glitter on the table. I

sink into one of the chairs and pick up a pen. What would a girl draw? A puppy? A bunch of flowers? A baby? A baby with a puppy and a bunch of flowers?

Then I see Sam is drawing a soccer jersey— Santos's soccer jersey!

I feel like Dan McGuire when he's pulled out of quicksand in *Dan*

McGuire and the Dunes of Doom.

"Hey, that's good."

"It'll be even better with glitter." Sam picks up the glue pen.

If she can do it, so can I. I set to work, dividing my card into squares and drawing the jersey of every first-division team. It turns out soccer jerseys look awesome in glitter.

By the time the rest of the girls come through, Sam and I have almost finished. It's a shame really—making cards is actually not a bad way to spend an afternoon.

"Lovely work, girls. Now, how about some snacks?"

Snacks are basically the same as any other birthday party—the same sandwiches (pointless), same chips, same carrot sticks (also pointless), same fruit. But Melissa's birthday cake is in the shape of a microphone and is covered with pink frosting. "For my little star," her mom says.

After snacks, Melissa gets all bouncy and giggly. She drags us into the living room and runs to the corner where a black box and a microphone have appeared. "Second surprise! We're doing karaoke!"

Everyone else laughs and grabs the song lists from Melissa's mom. Nerida's already doing that circle thing with her hips.

I take a step back toward the kitchen. "I can't do it." I'm hoping Sam will agree with me and suggest doing more glitter soccer jerseys. But she doesn't.

"Come on, Josie," she says, "you can't be allergic to singing."

"I'm not a very good singer."

"Neither am I. It doesn't matter. It's just about having fun." Sam gives me an odd look and I realize I have to go along with it so that she doesn't get suspicious.

From this point on, things get hazy—like a nightmare when you skip from scene to scene. Melissa sings something that has "Ooo baby, baby" in it over and over again. Then Nerida sings something by Lady Gaga and Sam sings something I've never heard of but involves her making sounds like dolphins calling each other in the wild. Then they're pushing me to the front and

"Mamma Mia" by Abba is blaring out. Abba! Eddie used to make fun of the girls for singing Abba in the playground after they'd all seen some film. I can just picture him, his hand over his mouth, bent over with laughter.

Nerida puts her arm around me and bumps her hip against mine. I croak out the words that are projected on the wall. I can hear my voice echoing in the mic. I sound like a sick frog. The other girls flick their hair around and bounce up and down on their feet. Melissa's mom is taking photos on her digital camera and she's promising to email copies to us.

Photos! Great. This isn't just the Afternoon of Shame, it could also put my identity at risk! Mom and Dad had better be ready to help destroy the evidence. This afternoon is completely their fault.

After Mom picks me up I refuse to speak to her for the rest of the evening. There's only one answer to her earlier question of "What's not to like?"

Everything.

For the next few days I try to distract myself from the memories of Melissa's party and the nightmares I have about being smothered in pink lip gloss and being forced to sing at a school assembly—alone. I put all my energy into spying on Mr. Caulfield. I reread my Dan McGuire books for tips and make notes on what I find out about Mr. Caulfield as soon as I get home. I search his desk at recess after I spill my pencil case on the floor accidently-on-purpose, and learn that:

- Mr. Caulfield has a habit of putting his coffee cup down on his lesson plans;
- Mr. Caulfield likes gardening. Evidence: a pile of seed packets in his drawer for tomatoes, carrots, spring onions, peas, and watercress; and
- Mr. Caulfield reads *Model Engineer, Model Boats,* and *Gardeners' World Magazine.*

It's not exactly the kind of high crime material I've been hoping for. After that promising conversation at the swimming pool, Mr. Caulfield is turning out to be just another ordinary teacher.

But Dan McGuire never gives up, so neither will I.

Chapter 10

When I come down to the kitchen on Friday morning, Mom is sitting at the table, surrounded by piles of paper with black lines blocking out most of the text.

"What's all this?" I pick up one of the pieces of paper.

Mom snatches it out of my hand. "Never mind. Go and get your cornflakes—you'll have to eat them in the living room."

"Why can't I eat them at the table?"

"I can't afford to take a chance of you seeing something you shouldn't."

I don't point out that since I don't have x-ray vision, that doesn't seem very likely. She's got her Serious Spy look on and I know not to question it. Really, there's no difference between her new Serious Spy look and her old Furious Mom expression. I get my bowl of cereal and go and sit on the sofa.

I bet most people don't have to worry about causing some kind of international crisis by eating their cornflakes in the wrong place. It's getting to be more and more important to prove to Mom and Dad that I'm up to being a real spy.

So when Mom goes upstairs to get dressed, I run into Mission Control to raid it again. Luckily, the one thing about Dad that has definitely not changed is that he leaves things in a mess. The spy gadgets are still in a jumble from when he was showing them to me—there's no way they'll notice anything's missing.

At lunchtime I make my way to the parking lot next to the playground. I've already waited to see

Mr. Caulfield arrive in his car, so I know he drives a blue Volvo. We're not supposed to go into the parking lot but there's a small side gate to it from the playground and I slip through it when no one is looking. I scoot down and run to the car, peering in the window. On the back seat is a dark blue bag with the logo BOTHEN HILL NEWS on it.

I look over my shoulder—no one's around—and I click the multi-remote I borrowed from Mission Control. There's a loud beep as the doors unlock. I wait a second and then pull the back door open.

I slip a voice-activated recording ruler on the floor under the passenger seat and then inch the bag open. I get a glimpse of a thick wad of papers and a folder that says ATTN: MARK RIAL.

Mr. Caulfield was talking to someone called Mark on the recording I made at the community pool! I know from Dan McGuire that you should keep infiltration time to a minimom so I'll have to make a separate plan for looking at the papers.

I click the door shut and relock the car, then run to the side gate and slip back into the playground. I've pulled my soccer ball out of my bag—if anyone's seen me come in I'll say I kicked my ball into the parking lot by accident.

I dribble the ball away from the gate and then lob it against the wall. Before I can get to it, Sam runs up and kicks it up onto her chest. She holds it in front of her. "This really is a great ball."

"Yeah, thanks." I hold out my hands for it.

But Sam's spun it around and is examining it. "Is this a faulty seam?" She peers closely at the part where the recording controls are.

"No. I mean, yes."

"There's a funny little dent here . . ."

I reach out for it but it's too late—we're listening to the recording of Mr. Caulfield's conversation.

I grab the ball and scrabble to find the off button—but not before Sam's heard the whole thing.

Sam looks at me as if I'm off my rocker. "I don't get it. You've got a soccer ball recorder and you recorded Mr. Caulfield?"

"It was by accident—when he confiscated my ball."

"But why have you got a *recording soccer ball*?"

I wish I could tell Sam the truth—all of it. She's been the one person who's made school bearable. But Dan McGuire's first rule is "Trust no one" and if she lets something slip, I could put my whole family in danger. I decide on a half-truth.

"Do you know the Dan McGuire books?"

"Sure. I got the box set for Christmas."

"You did?"

Eddie was never interested in Dan McGuire. He thought reading was boring. So Sam liking him as well is totally awesome. I'm about to ask her what her favorite book is when she taps my soccer ball.

"So? What's that got to do with you having recording equipment?"

"Oh. Well. Yeah. I read them all the time. So my mom and dad have always given me presents to do with spies."

"Like this ball?"

"Yeah. Lots of stuff like that. And I heard this conversation and thought I'd practice my spying skills by checking it out."

"That recording must have to do with Mr. Caulfield doing the accounts for school," Sam says. "I remember my mom said how nice he was for offering. She says doing the accounts for anything is a real pain."

"I know it doesn't sound likely, but I don't think he was being nice." I take out the recording pen and play her the conversation from the swimming pool. It's a bit harder to hear him on that one because of all the background splashing but you can get the gist. "You see what I mean? It's a bit suspicious."

"Maybe, but my mom's a reporter," Sam tells me, "and she always says you have to have *loads* of evidence before you can prove something."

"Do you want to help me see if there is any?" It's risky involving Sam, but I'm tired of being on my own all the time. Besides, now that she knows about the gadgets, it'll be hard to hide what I'm doing from her in any case.

Sam shakes her head. "I can't believe Mr. Caulfield would do anything wrong. He doesn't even look like a criminal."

"I know—but the best ones never do." In the True Stories section of *Dan McGuire and the Acid Armour*, there's a part about a spy called James Rivington who ran a coffee shop. Would you suspect the person who sold you a latte?

Sam hesitates for a second. "And you have lots of spy equipment?"

"Tons." At least I don't have to lie about that.

"I guess it would be fun to do a bit of real spying," she says. "But it doesn't mean I think he's guilty."

"Great." Even if I can't tell her all my secrets, it's a relief to be able to share my mission with Sam. What's the fun of having genius gadgets if you have to do the investigation alone?

For someone who isn't even sure if Mr. Caulfield is guilty or not, Sam really gets into the whole spy mission idea. She says we should call it

Operation Numbered because if I'm right about Mr. Caulfield committing a crime then his teaching days are numbered. "And," she says, "we might get a substitute teacher in for the rest of the semester—and they *never* give homework!"

On the bus home, I tell Sam about the recording ruler and the bag in the back of Mr. Caulfield's car with the papers I saw.

"We could do a bag swap so we can take photos of whatever's in there. You've got a camera, right?"

"Yeah, but how do we get another BOTHEN HILL NEWS bag?"

Sam laughs. "Easy. They gave out lots of them to promote the paper. I told you. My mom's a reporter—she *works* for *Bothen Hill News*. We've got about ten of them at home."

"Excellent!"

By the time we reach my house we've worked out the details of the first stage of Operation Numbered. "Do you want me to come in so we can make some more plans?" asks Sam.

"Uh, no, better not. I'm not allowed to bring

anyone home without telling my parents first." I'm not allowed to bring anyone home at all—and this is the first time I've minded.

"Can't you just run in and tell them now?"

"No, they work really hard and they get . . . really tired so they like to know, you know, way in advance." If I was Pinocchio, my nose would be in Australia by now.

"I see," Sam says. She glances up at my house and then back at me with an odd look on her face.

It's definitely time to change the subject. "So, is your dad a reporter as well?"

"No. It's just me and my mom—my dad left years ago. Anyway, I'll go home and dig out one of those bags for Monday."

"Great. And, uh, maybe you can come over another time." My Pinocchio nose has made it to New Zealand.

It's hard not to think about how much easier life would be if Mom and Dad *weren't* undercover spies.

Chapter 11

At the end of assembly on Monday, Mrs. Harrison makes an announcement.

"I'm sure we're all aware of how well our girls' soccer team has been doing in the school league. As you may know, our next match will be between our own team here at Bothen Hill and the girls at St. Colmer's. But Mr. Caulfield has managed to arrange something rather exciting. The game will take place at the local *professional* soccer field!"

An excited murmur starts up. "And this won't be just any game. A local journalist has agreed to cover the match!"

"That'll be my mom!" Sam whispers to me.

Mrs. Harrison holds up her hand for quiet. "The reason for this is that we will be raising money and awareness for a very worthy cause that Mr. Caulfield has brought to our attention—the charity Start Sports. As you know, we usually support charities like the Red Cross and Oxfam with our school events, but this semester we are happy to give our fund-raising power to a new charity that is clearly very dear to Mr. Caulfield. So I hope everyone here will do their part to contribute to this exciting project—whether it's by playing on the team, collecting donations, or getting your friends and family to come along."

I've got two thoughts in my head.

1. If this has anything to do with that conversation of Mr. Caulfield's and it turns out he's doing something criminal with this charity, then I now officially hate Mr. Caulfield.

2. A chance to play on a professional soccer field! Covered by a real journalist! I love Mr. Caulfield!

The bell rings and everyone files out. Melissa and Nerida are already talking about getting their picture in the local paper.

As soon as we're in the hall, Sam nudges me. "Come to the bathroom."

"Why?"

"Because it's a good place to talk, idiot."

That's one mystery cleared up.

In the bathroom, Sam checks all the stalls before speaking. "Didn't Mr. Caulfield say something on that swimming recording about a charity?"

"That's exactly what I was thinking." I take out the pen and play it back to her. "There's definitely something weird about this. We should look it up on the Internet."

"Okay, come back to my house after school," says Sam. "But we get the ruler and do the bag swap first."

It feels pretty great to have a real spy schedule. This must be what it's like when Mom and Dad talk to each other.

But the first stage of Operation Numbered doesn't go as planned. In fact, it doesn't go at all. At first recess, Sam and I head over to the parking lot with the replacement bag tucked under Sam's arm, but as we come up to the gate, Sam swivels away from it and waves me back. "He's in the car!"

We move as fast as we can so that we're not in view of the gate.

"I bet he's calling someone." Then I remember what's in the car. "That means another recording!"

"Operation Numbered will be relaunched at lunchtime," Sam says.

I smile back at her. "Right."

We eat as fast as we can and are out in the playground before anyone else. Unfortunately, so is Mr. Caulfield.

"I'll keep him talking." Sam thrusts the bag at me. "You get the ruler and do the switch."

"What are you going to talk to him about?" I hiss.

"Our chances against St. Colmer's." Sam grins. "And how amazing my mom's article will be."

I sprint over to the gate and then look over my shoulder. Sam's managed to get Mr. Caulfield facing her, so his back is to me. She tugs her ear— our signal for *go ahead*—and I slip through into the parking lot before anyone notices me.

I unlock Mr. Caulfield's car and put my hand down under the passenger seat to pick up the ruler. As I feel around for it, I touch a piece of paper that's dropped onto the floor. I glance at it and see the words START SPORTS across the top. I stuff it into my bag and then find the ruler wedged under the mat. I'm about to pull out the BOTHEN HILL NEWS bag that Sam's given me when I hear voices—Mrs. Harrison and another teacher—discussing a staff meeting. I click the car door shut and crouch down, crawling around the side of the car so that I'm hidden from view and then lying flat on the pavement. From underneath the car I see their feet disappearing through the gate. The gate swings shut after them but they don't move away! They stay there, chatting.

I can't risk doing the bag swap now. But I have to get back into school before anyone realizes I'm gone. I crouch-run to the parking lot exit and lock the car before running along the pavement back to the front entrance to the school. A teaching assistant is on duty at the gate and when I tell her I've been gathering the packed lunch that I'd forgotten from my mom, she just waves me through.

"Where've you been?" Sam runs up to me. "Did you do it?"

"Only the ruler, not the bag. But don't worry, I've got an idea. I'll just have to bring in more gadgets."

Sam raises her eyebrows. "Good thing you're so well supplied."

"I'd better put my bag back." As a spy, you have to know how to deflect danger. In my case, that seems to mean changing the subject. A lot.

At soccer practice Mr. Caulfield says I can be on the team for the match against St Colmer's. I'm not even an alternate!

Everything's perfect until we have a break halfway through. I slump down next to Sam and don't notice my tracksuit bottoms have bunched up and my socks have rolled down. I only realize this when I see Sam staring—at my unusually hairy ankles. At my *incredibly-not-girly* hairy ankles.

"It's funny that you have dark hair on your legs when you're blonde," she says, looking at me closely.

I thought she was going to say something about my legs being hairy—put-on-a-leash-and-take-for-a-walk hairy.

"Uh, yeah. It runs in the family. Different colored hair."

"I thought maybe you'd dyed it."

"Course not!" My laugh doesn't sound that convincing. But that's because it's hard to sound like you think something's funny when you're terrified.

Sam puts her head to one side and studies my face.

"What is it?" I ask, not meeting her eyes.

"I don't know," she says. "Sometimes you remind me of something but I don't know what it is." She stands up. "Come on, Mr. Caulfield's about to blow the whistle."

I follow her onto the field, pushing down the panicky feeling in my stomach. I wonder if what Sam's being reminded of is *boy*, and what she senses is the something that tells you what you're looking at isn't really what it seems to be. If Sam is already starting to guess, how long do I have before everyone else does? Have my hairy ankles put our lives in danger?

Chapter 12

As soon as we're on the bus I pull out the piece of paper I found on the floor of Mr. Caulfield's car. Underneath the START SPORTS heading are various logos—a soccer ball being held up by kids, a tennis racket held by a large hand, a drawing of a girl in the starting position for a sprint. Then START SPORTS typed in lots of different fonts. Underneath all that is an official-looking list of the Start Sports charity team. It's short. Very short. There's only one name: Mr. N. Caulfield, Chief Executive.

"Mrs. Harrison didn't say anything about Mr. Caulfield being part of the charity." Sam draws a circle in the fogged-up window.

"Maybe she doesn't know."

We look at each other. Operation Numbered has moved up a gear.

I text Mom to let her know I'm going to Sam's. I'm a bit nervous about meeting Sam's mom in case she's like Melissa's mom and tries to give me some kind of makeover. But she hardly looks up from her computer. She just smiles, gives us a brief wave, and tells us to help ourselves to cookies. Her fingers are typing at about a million miles a minute.

"She wants to be promoted," Sam tells me as we go upstairs. "So, she covers every story she can. But it's all stuff like the village fête or how local shops are being closed down. She needs a big story to get her noticed."

"Maybe we'll be able to give it to her."

Sam grins at me and pushes open the door to her room. The walls are pale green and there's a dark green side table next to the bed. The curtains and comforter are both covered in some red and white spotty material and she has lots of posters of soccer players.

"This is your room?" It can't be! It's normal!

"What's wrong with it?" Sam looks offended. "You don't like it?"

"No, no, it's great. But it's—it's not pink."

"Why would it be?"

"I just thought all girls . . ."

"What? That all girls like pink?" Sam raises her eyebrows. "You really think that?"

"No. Of course I don't." Yes, of course I do. "Come on, let's listen to the new recording." I make a big thing out of looking through my bag for the ruler even though I know exactly where I put it. By the time I pull it out, Sam seems to have forgotten about the pink comment. At least, I hope she has.

Even though it's voice-activated, the recorder isn't so great that it picks up when people are having boring instead of important conversations. We have to listen to ten minutes of Mr. Caulfield calling a plumber for his leaking toilet and then calling a local gardening center to find out what kind of vegetables are easiest to grow in a hot, dry climate.

"But where we live *isn't* hot and dry!" Sam points out.

Finally, we get to a conversation worth listening to.

"Recording started 10:31 a.m., Monday," says the recorder.

"That's first recess today!" I say. "I knew he must be calling someone from the car."

There's a beep and then Mr. Caulfield's voice. "Mark, I've got the bank statements and the Start Sports papers. You're sure you can clean them up?"

We can't really hear the other voice except as fuzzy static.

"Excellent. I've been doing very well with the grant-funding applications—everyone loves the idea of Start Sports," Mr. Caulfield's voice says. "Encouraging healthy habits and community participation in sports—they're practically falling over themselves to give cash. And the soccer match will raise even more."

More fuzzy static.

"I'll bring the papers in tomorrow and meet you after school. I want this figured out ASAP. Once the cash is all in the bank, why hang around?"

"Recording ended: 10:34 a.m., Monday," the recorder says before clicking off.

"We have to get ahold of those papers tomorrow," says Sam. "Before he gives them to what'shisface."

"Definitely. But let's see what we can find out online."

"Oh, yeah." Sam turns on a laptop and types *Start Sports* into Google.

There are a lot of links for starting stuff—diets, fitness routines, new jobs—and a lot of links for sports—football, soccer, basketball—but there's nothing about a charity called Start Sports.

"It doesn't exist," Sam says. "He's made up a charity to get people to give money to it. That means he's taking money away from the Red Cross and Oxfam, too, because we usually raise money for them."

"And it sounds like he's running off after the match." I think for a second. "I bet he's going somewhere that has a hot, dry climate."

Sam scowls at the laptop as she shuts it down. "We've got to stop him."

Getting back into Mission Control that night isn't a problem. Dad's left to do the shopping and Mom's taking a bath after a long, hard day of surveillance. I pick up the disrupter and a couple of other things I think might come in handy the next day. In my old life, I used to know where Mom and Dad's chocolate stash was. In my new life, everything's been turned up a notch and I know where their spy gadget stash is. After working with Sam earlier, I almost feel like a real spy—and then I go into my room and see that my new dresses have arrived. *My new dresses.* They're not frilly and they're not pink, but Dad's clearly making his girly girl point with the accessories. There are pink sparkly hair clips in the shape of a rabbit, a kitten, a puppy, and a duck. They remind me that even though I have a spy mission, I am still dressing up as a girl. A girl with a small animal obsession.

I have to play an hour of Mega Tank on my phone before I feel even *close* to normal.

"You've got a pretty amazing collection of spy stuff," Sam says the next morning on the bus after I've given her a glimpse inside my bag. "You got it all from your parents?"

"No. Some of it I got with my allowance. You know, online."

That's the problem with lies. It's a bit like hiccups—once you start, it's hard to stop.

"You're funny," Sam says. "You *look* like the kind of girl Melissa is, but you don't *act* the same way girls like her usually do."

"Haven't you ever heard of not judging a book by its cover?"

"You're not a book."

"Yes, I am. I'm the girl version of Dan McGuire."

She laughs, but all I can think is, *How long until she knows?*

I try not to worry about it. I need to focus.

Today, we're not taking any chances. We need two distractions, one so we can do the swap and the other so we can put the original bag back.

At first recess, we take our positions. I sit on one of the benches by the main gate and select the fire alarm function on the disrupter in my backpack and then tuck the backpack under the bench. I get up and walk away from the bench with the remote control in my hand.

I look over at Sam and tug my ear. She nods.

I flick the switch on the remote and as the disrupter starts to shriek, Sam sprints off to the parking lot.

Everyone pours out of the building. Some people are shouting "Fire!" and some are laughing, and a couple of kids are in tears. Mrs. Harrison is hurrying through the playground with her phone glued to her ear while the other teachers organize everyone in lines. As Mr. Caulfield arrives to tick people off the attendance list, I flick the alarm off and quickly retrieve my backpack from under the bench. A second later, Sam's back, panting.

"Done?"

She turns to show the bag slung over her shoulder. "Done."

We stuff it into my backpack and join the line for our class.

Mrs. Harrison reappears, frowning. "I don't understand, why has it just *stopped*? I was about to call the fire department."

We have to stand around for a long time while the teachers are talking about how the alarm didn't sound like the usual one and whether it's safe to go back inside. Then the janitor appears and insists that the school fire alarm didn't go off at all. At last they decide that it must have been from the house next door to the school and after a while we all file back inside. Stage one of Operation Numbered is complete.

At lunch, while Sam keeps a lookout, I lock myself in a bathroom stall and photograph every document in Mr. Caulfield's bag with one of Mom and Dad's miniature cameras. Mr. Caulfield's bank

statement shows lots and lots of entries under the deposit heading—all from Bothen Hill School. His total balance is over six hundred thousand dollars! And there's another bank statement in the name of Start Sports—and the only contact listed is Mr. Caulfield. I think we've got our proof now. As soon as I'm finished, I stuff the papers back in the bag and come out.

"Okay, let's put it back."

I show Sam the disrupter and how to operate it. She whistles. "I'm starting to think I shouldn't spend all my allowance on chocolate."

This time, we've decided on fireworks. Sam is setting the disrupter off in one of the bathrooms so that everyone assumes they can't see the fireworks because they're going off inside. I get out into the playground and as close as I can to the parking lot before she sets it off. At the first fizz and bang, I dash through the gate. Everyone turns and surges into school to find out what the noise is about. I unlock the car and do the bag swap in seconds. I'm almost out of the parking lot when I smack straight into Mr. Caulfield.

My heart leapfrogs in my chest. "Hello, sir."

"Josie. What are you doing here?" Mr. Caulfield is staring at his car.

"I heard all that noise in the school and it scared me. I guess I just ran." I sound completely convincing. I used to be horrible at lying, but Josie is getting really good at it.

Except that Mr. Caulfield doesn't look very convinced. He keeps glancing over at the car and then at me. "What's that key for, Josie?"

I'm still holding the multi-remote key! What was I thinking?

"It's my mom's. She lost it yesterday after she dropped me off."

"I thought you said you ran here because you were scared?

And how did your mom drive her car if she lost her key?"

Okay, maybe I need a bit of work on the lying front.

"She always keeps a spare in her bag because she loses it a lot. I ran here because I was scared and then saw the key."

"I see." Mr. Caulfield keeps looking from me to the car. "That's an interesting bag, Josie. I've got one just like it."

I take a deep breath. I have to stay calm, just like Dan McGuire would. "Yeah, Sam gave it to me. Her mom works for the *Bothen Hill News*."

"So she does."

There's this long, heart-beats-in-your-throat pause. After what feels like hours, Mr. Caulfield says, "Well, I think you'd better go back to the playground now. Whatever that noise was, it's over."

"Okay, sir. Thanks." And then I *run*.

Not every spy mission can be expected to go perfectly.

Chapter 13

On the bus, I tell Sam what I saw in the bag.

"I can't believe he's really stealing all that money!" Sam's turned red in the face. "I *hate* liars. My dad was a liar. He lied about having an affair and Mom cried for about six months. We've got to show everyone what Mr. Caulfield's really like. Who he really is."

It makes me think of Sam finding out who *I* really am. If she hates liars, would she hate me?

I stop myself from thinking about it by telling her my idea of how to expose Mr. Caulfield. Sam loves it. "We're really going to stop him!"

It's only when I'm back at home that I start to worry. What if I didn't get the papers back in order and Mr. Caulfield realizes for sure that we're onto him? What if he tries to find out stuff about me—and he finds out about Mom and Dad and who we really are?

Though I can't help thinking that if we're captured, at least I wouldn't have to wear a skirt.

"You all right?" Dad peers at me across the table at dinner. "Anything wrong at school? Did you see anything suspicious?"

I think about telling them everything but decide I won't unless I'm sure I've put us all in danger. If Sam and I can prove what Mr. Caulfield is up to, Mom and Dad will have to realize I can spy like them. But maybe I should find out the consequences if we do get uncovered . . . just in case.

"If we are found out—about us not being who we're saying we are, I mean—could we be killed?"

"*Killed?*" Mom laughs. "No, of course not! We would never be killed." She puts her hand on top of mine and gives it a squeeze.

"Maybe sent to another country for a while," says Dad.

"Or detained in a security facility for a bit," adds Mom.

I want to be a professional soccer player in Brazil! That's not going to happen in a security facility!

"But no, we wouldn't be killed," Dad says cheerfully.

My parents are such a comfort.

The next morning we're at school extra early to make sure we complete the next stage of our mission before attendance. Luckily Mrs. Harrison is already in and she loves our plan. She thinks we have "initiative" and are full of "community spirit." All we have to do is go to the classroom and wait.

Mr. Caulfield's finished taking attendance when Mrs. Harrison taps lightly at the door.

"Mr. Caulfield? May I come in a moment?"

"Of course, Mrs. Harrison, come in, come in."

"Josie and Sam were kind enough to let me tell you the wonderful news myself," Mrs. Harrison says.

"News? What news is that, Mrs. Harrison?"

You can see from the way his eyes dart around the room that he's getting nervous.

"Your two students have come up with the wonderful idea of making a film about Start Sports! I'm making arrangements for it to be shown at the stadium before the game. Such initiative!"

Mr. Caulfield doesn't say anything. He looks as if someone's rubbed ice all over his face.

"So, of course they'll be wanting to talk to you, as you know so much about the charity. And perhaps you could even set up a few interviews with some of the people who actually run it?"

Mr. Caulfield's still not speaking.

"Mr. Caulfield?"

Mr. Caulfield clears his throat. "I think it might be difficult to set up the interviews with Start Sports in time—I mean, the match is in just a couple of days."

"Oh, surely they'll find someone to talk to us when we're doing so much to help highlight all they do and stand for? We'll be raising a lot of money for them after all!" Mrs. Harrison sends Mr. Caulfield another positive smile.

"They're a very small charity," he says quickly. "Just starting out. Small team, you know."

"Oh. Well, I'm sure the girls can make do with an extra-long interview with you if that's the case."

"The thing is, I don't know when I'll be free, what with teaching, lesson-planning, grading, coaching the team for the match . . ."

"Oh, Mr. Caulfield, *surely* you can spare just a few minutes for the girls? Josie and Sam have already gone to a lot of trouble to borrow filming and recording equipment. And after all, it is for *charity*."

Mr. Caulfield glances at the door as if he's considering making a run for it. "Yes, all right then. Maybe we can do the interview at lunchtime. I'll be able to talk to the girls then."

"Excellent! Come to my office and I'll just hide myself away in a corner while you have the interview. I'm eager to hear all about this charity myself—as you've said, it's brand new!" Mrs. Harrison laughs. "Now, I must let you get on with your lessons, everyone."

She disappears and Mr. Caulfield stares after her as if he's just been given some terrible news. Which he has, really.

It's just as well I've done my last Mission Control raid for this operation. I heard Mom ask Dad this morning if he's been rearranging the gadget shelves. Still, it will all be worth it when we pull this off.

Mr. Caulfield sits on a chair in Mrs. Harrison's room for the interview, looking exactly like someone in one of the court dramas Dad used to watch—guilty.

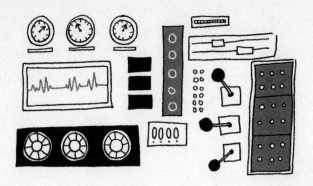

Mrs. Harrison watches from the corner with a big smile on her face, already nodding in approval even though no one's said anything yet.

Sam positions the video camera and presses RECORD. "So. When exactly did you find out about Start Sports, Mr. Caulfield?"

"Um. I think I saw something about it in one of the soccer magazines."

"And can you tell us a bit about how it works and why it's a good charity? Why we should be giving money to Start Sports instead of to the Red Cross and Oxfam?"

"Yes, well . . ." Mr. Caulfield coughs. "It's about encouraging kids and adults to play sports, and, you know, take part in the community."

I resume the questioning. "By playing sports?"

"Yeah. That's right." Mr. Caulfield nods several times like those bobbing-head toy dogs people put in the back of their cars.

"So, they organize games, then?"

"Uh, yeah. That's right." Mr. Caulfield does some more nodding. Behind the camera, I see Sam trying to hide a smile.

"Where?"

"What?" Mr. Caulfield shifts nervously in his seat.

"Where do they organize these games? I mean, because I'd really like to get involved."

"The thing is," Mr. Caulfield says, glancing at the camera, "the charity's only just been put together. So, you know, some of this stuff hasn't happened yet."

"Like the games."

"Yeah."

"So, at the moment, they don't actually do anything."

"Um, well." Mr. Caulfield coughs. "As I said, things are at an early stage."

I press on. "You mean they haven't done any charity work yet."

Mr. Caulfield coughs again, his skin slowly turning a deep purple. "Not as yet, not as such . . . no." Confirmation—goal!

Mrs. Harrison laughs. "Now, Josie. Sorry, Sam, if you'd just like to put it on pause a moment."

"Oh, it doesn't matter, Miss, you can be in the film, too." Sam swings the camera over to her.

Mrs. Harrison touches her hair. "Oh. Well. As Mr. Caulfield was saying, the charity has just been created. That's exciting in itself. After all, we as a school can be said to be helping it on its first steps—can't we, Mr. Caulfield?"

"Yeah, that's right." He's definitely sounding a bit queasy now.

"And who thought of it?" Sam smiles encouragingly. "Who's the person behind it all?"

This is the question we've been working toward. I think of the charity account statement with only Mr. Caulfield's name on it. If Mr. Caulfield lies now, we've got him for sure. I hold my breath.

Mr. Caulfield stares at Sam for a long second. "Do you mean who runs it?"

"Yeah, runs it, had the idea, organizes everything. You know."

"Uh . . . right. Well. It's a woman called . . ." Mr. Caulfield's eyes dart around the room. I see him stare at the clock over the door.

"Lesley Clock. Yeah, her name is Lesley Clock."

Goal!

"Lesley *Clock*?" I have to bite the inside of my mouth to stop myself from laughing.

"Yeah, that's right." A drop of sweat forms on his forehead, and he reaches up to wipe it off.

"That's an unusual name," Sam says, throwing me a quick smile. "So, who else runs it?"

Mr. Caulfield forces out a laugh. "Well, I can't know everything about the charity, you know, Sam—I don't run it myself!"

Hat-trick!

"I think that's enough for now, in any case," Mrs. Harrison says. "The bell's going to ring in a moment and we must allow Mr. Caulfield *some* time off for good behavior!"

Sam and I exchange a look. If the rest of our mission goes to plan, Mrs. Harrison is going to find out all about Mr. Caulfield's behavior . . .

Chapter 14

"Okay, go and get changed for gym, everyone."
Mr. Caulfield sounds a bit snappy but that's to be
expected. Criminals do get jittery when they're
under attack. It's how Dan McGuire always knows
he's on the right track.

I'm heading down the hall when Mr. Caulfield
calls after me. "Where are you going, Josie?"

"Just to the bathroom, sir."

"There's a bathroom next to the changing
room."

Up to now, I've gotten away with changing in the bathroom farthest away from the changing room, and apart from the one walk-through at the community pool, I've managed to avoid the whole getting-undressed-in-front-of-other-people question altogether. I'm about to play my shy card when I see the look in Mr. Caulfield's eye. He's not in the mood to be understanding.

"Come on, Josie. Get moving."

It's too bad we're not doing track today. I am so ready to run.

I'm in for a shock when I get to the changing room. The bathroom next to it has a large sign hanging on the door—OUT OF ORDER. I feel a bubble of panic rise up in me. I turn to try and go back to the other bathroom but now I'm surrounded by girls, all talking and laughing as they push through the changing room door.

"Come on, Josie, get a move on!" Melissa pulls at my sleeve.

I've got no choice but to follow her. As soon as I'm inside, I realize this isn't gym; it's biology.

"Are you all right?" Sam slings her bag on the hook over the bench.

"Fine." I look around desperately. Where's the stall for shy girls to change in? There's nowhere to hide. It's like one of those nature programs when they film the prey of a predator in the wild. And guess who's the deer staring into the lion's massive mouth?

Sam starts pulling off her sweater. No! Not Sam!

My skin feels like it's been lit with a match. I keep my eyes down and try to ignore what's happening around me. Everyone is tugging off skirts and tops and tights. Everyone's flinging clothes around and chatting as if it's all perfectly normal. Nerida's not just talking about her bra, but she's getting everyone to *look at it* and tell her how pretty it is. What's *wrong* with her? Boys don't go around getting people to admire their underpants! I keep my eyes locked on my bag and take out my tracksuit bottoms. At least I won't have to change my top as I have a long-sleeved T-shirt under my school sweater. Why didn't Mom and Dad plan for this?! What kind of spies do they think they are? They can't even protect their son from having to get changed in front of millions of girls!

I can't think of one single situation that Dan McGuire's ever faced that's worse than this. That bit in *Dan McGuire and the Fiery Flames* when he has to walk through a burning building that's been doused in gasoline? Or *Dan McGuire and the Rasp of the Rattle* when he's dropped into a cauldron of snakes? Or when he has to dive under an ice floe and swim away from a pod of killer whales? Nothing. *Nothing* compared to this.

"Josie? Are you okay?" Melissa peers into my face. Great, now everyone's looking at me.

"I'm fine. Just—I'm just—" *About to throw up.*

 Melissa goes away and I wriggle out of my tights without taking off my skirt. Then I lean over and yank up my tracksuit bottoms before anyone can get a load of my hairy legs.

"Whoa! Josie!"

Oh no. Here we go. Deportation city. The cover's blown. Someone's seen the giveaway legs and put them together and added up to JOSIE'S A *BOY*. What's going to happen to me and Mom and Dad? I've ruined everything!

Someone's hand tugs at my exposed waistband. "Boxer shorts?!"

I twist around to see Nerida's mouth stretched out in a delighted grin. "*Boxer* shorts?! I've seen boxer-style *panties* but these are *real* boxers. You must be totally boy crazy!"

I tug down my T-shirt. I'd like to say something clever, but my brain's on strike.

"Don't you know anything, Nerida?" Sam appears in front of me. "Boxers are the new thing. My mom's doing a piece about film stars wearing their boyfriends' boxers in the paper. It's *huge* in Hollywood," she says.

I stay very still.

Nerida's grin freezes. "Oh."

"Yeah. Surprised none of you knew about it."

"Why aren't *you* wearing them, then?" asks Nerida.

Shut up, bra-face.

"Just waiting for them to arrive," Sam says casually. "My mom ordered me some online on Saturday."

"Oh."

It's the "oh" of defeat. It's the sound of that "oh" that makes me realize my boy butt is saved.

"That's so cool!" Melissa says. "I'll get some over the weekend!"

"Me, too!"

And suddenly there's a chorus of voices, all talking about how they're going to get themselves some boxer shorts as soon as they can.

Sam's saved me from discovery and created a new fashion craze all at the same time.

But do I thank her? Do I even look at her as we make our way out of the changing room and into the playground? No, I do not. Not because I'm not grateful. I am. I realize how good a friend Sam is more every day. How much I'll miss her if I get taken away with Mom and Dad. No, it's not because I don't want to thank her that I'm not looking at her. It's because I'm wondering why she covered up for me as if she knew what I've got to hide.

Sam doesn't talk to me during gym. She doesn't talk to me in the changing room. She doesn't talk to me while we work on our history project, Exploring the Vikings, or when the bell rings for the end of school. She doesn't talk to me on the bus or when we get off.

But just outside my house she whips around to face me.

"You're a boy, aren't you?"

I give it one last try. "What?!"

"You're a boy disguised as a girl."

"You're crazy."

"Hairy ankles, boxer shorts, big feet. Allergic to water and makeup. Loves soccer and Mega Tank but wears sparkly *bunny rabbit* clips in her hair and thinks girls only like pink.

How likely is that?"

"Everyone's different!"

Sam looks at me. "Shall I give that hair a tug?"

"No!" I slam a hand to the top of my head to protect myself. It's bad enough that Sam's guessed, but if she says anything, or if anyone else does . . .

"I thought maybe it was true but I wasn't sure. Even though there were so many signs, I trusted you. That was stupid, wasn't it?" She looks away, chewing on her bottom lip.

I step toward her even though she immediately backs away. "No, you see, there's a reason—but I can't tell you what it is. But it's really important, Sam, you have to believe me."

"I don't care what the reason is. I. Don't. Like. Liars." Sam takes another step back.

"Sam, wait!"

She puts her hands on her hips. "What did you do it for? A bet? A dare? A joke?"

"You've got to be kidding me. You think I'd do it for a joke? Why would I *want* to be a girl?"

Sam narrows her eyes. "What's so bad about

being a girl?"

"Nothing. Nothing!"

Sam stares at me as if she doesn't know me.

"Let me explain." I don't know what I'm going to say. I can't tell her the truth, but I hate seeing the expression in Sam's eyes. Like she can't stand to look at me.

"I don't want to talk to you right now." Sam's eyes well up. "What kind of friend lies to you like that? What kind of friend do you think you are?" She spins around on her heel and runs off.

Every day I've been thinking that having to dress up as a girl is the worst thing that's ever happened to me. As I watch Sam slam the door of her house behind her, suddenly I'm not so sure.

Chapter 15

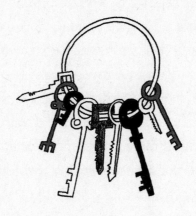

I work until really late on the Start Sports documentary. I can at least make sure that the rest of Operation Numbered goes to plan, even if my real mission has failed. I try to convince myself Sam won't give me away. If she covered up for me in gym, doesn't that mean she understands that it's important—even if she doesn't know why? But if she *does* tell . . . we'll be in real danger. My stomach churns as I put the film together.

When Eddie and I used to have fights, we'd shout and maybe push each other around. Sometimes we might not speak to each other for an hour, but it didn't usually last because we'd get bored or forget why we were annoyed. Mind you, we would be arguing about which one of us was better at soccer, or whether Lays are better than Pringles, or which was the best ever episode of *Doctor Who*. We never had an argument about one of us pretending to be something they weren't. Like a girl. So maybe it's normal that I'm a lot more bothered than I ever was when Eddie and I had a fight.

Sam likes the same stuff I do and doesn't make fun of me all the time like Eddie did. She doesn't boast about the stuff she's good at the way he did. And she's stuck by me and gotten me out of trouble even though she didn't have to.

She's been a better friend to me than Eddie ever was, and now I've messed it up.

Of course, Sam isn't at the bus stop the next morning. She must have left early or got her mom to give her a ride. I don't see her until I get into class, and when I sit down she doesn't look at me once.

I find her in the hall at recess. "Can I talk to you for a second?"

"Do you want to go in here, or there?" Sam jerks her head toward the boys' bathroom.

"Shhh, please." I glance around to see if anyone's heard her. This could be disastrous. I could be on my way to some high-security facility with Mom and Dad by this afternoon—or worse—if Sam decides to tell everyone. I tug at her sleeve and lead her into the girls' bathroom. Luckily, it's empty.

Sam leans against the sink and folds her arms across her chest. "What do you want?"

"I'm really sorry I lied to you. You've got to believe me, I'm not doing this because I want to. It's because I have to."

"You *have* to lie?"

"It's not just me. It's my mom and dad, too."

"What—your mom's a man and your dad's a woman?"

"No! I mean we'd all be in danger if it got out

that I'm not a girl."

Sam just raises an eyebrow.

This isn't going well. I appeal to her sense of justice.

"What about Operation Numbered? We need to make sure everyone knows what Mr. Caulfield's done."

"Oh. Right. We have to uncover Mr. Caulfield's lies. But it's okay for *you* to lie."

"But I'm not stealing anything from anyone! I'm not hurting anyone by dressing like a girl!"

"No? What about *me*?"

The bell rings and Sam walks out of the bathroom without another word.

I end up with Melissa and Nerida and Suzy in the playground at lunchtime. I watch Sam kicking a soccer ball and wish I could join in.

"Did you have a fight with Sam?" Nerida hops up on the wall and swings her legs.

"Well, obviously she did," Melissa says. She gives me a sympathetic look. "What was it about, Josie? Maybe we can help."

"Nothing. I mean, I don't know."

"Do you want to come over after school? We could do each other's nails and watch *Dancing with the Stars*."

"Thanks, but I can't." I don't mention I'd rather be left in a zoo's lion enclosure covered in raw steak.

Mr. Caulfield is off during the afternoon. Mrs. Harrison says he's got a lot to organize before the match tomorrow. I can't help glancing over at Sam when she says that. I bet he's booking his flight to Mexico or the Canaries or wherever he's decided to run away to with his stolen money. But Sam keeps looking straight ahead.

It's weird, because ever since I've had to dress like a girl, I haven't wanted anyone to look at me, and now Sam won't and I'd do anything to make her turn around.

I can't even think of a situation that Dan

McGuire has been in that's like this. Probably because Dan McGuire doesn't have any friends.

He should. Everyone needs one.

I've basically given up when Sam comes over to me after school at the bus stop.

"I'm not going to tell anyone about you." She holds up her hand before I can say anything. "But I won't help you with Operation Numbered unless you do the right thing at the match."

"What do you mean?"

"That's what you've got to figure out."

"What—"

"That's all you get. See you later." Sam stalks past me, leaving me staring after her.

I have absolutely no idea what she wants me to do.

Chapter 16

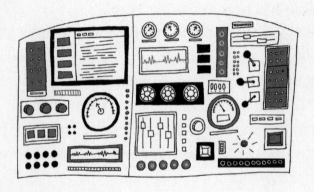

I don't think I've ever slept so badly—not even the first night after I found out I had to become "Josephine." I keep thinking about the plan and what will happen if it goes wrong—which it will if I can't figure out what Sam wants me to do. But it's not just the operation going wrong that I'm worried about. If I don't get Sam to forgive me, she won't be my friend again, and if she won't be my friend again, then I really can't stand this Josie cover any more. It's like that thing about how every dog year is seven human years. Every Josie day is like a year of my old life.

And then, just as it's getting light, I get it. It's not so much like a lightbulb flashing as being washed all over in sunlight. I can't believe it took me so long to figure it out! It's a good punishment, too. But it's worth it if it means Sam will be on my side again.

Now I can enjoy every minute of the day, every minute of exposing Mr. Caulfield for the fraud he is—while *my* fraud stays securely hidden under my skirt.

I spring out of bed to check the weather—the one thing we can't control is a cancellation because of rain. But the sunshine's flooding into my room. For the first time I don't even mind fixing my wig and putting on my skirt and tights. Josie's not so bad. After all, without her, none of this would be about to happen.

The match has been scheduled for late morning, so when I get to school the team is already boarding the bus that Mrs. Harrison's organized.

Everyone's chattering like mad. I don't manage to get a seat next to Sam so I can't tell her I know what to do. I do flash her a grin, though. She looks away, but I can tell she wants to smile back. That's the thing about friends—you have a secret code. Just like spies do.

The stadium is amazing. The field—a professional field!—is so green it's practically shining. I can't help imagining what it would be like to score a goal in a stadium like this.

As everyone marvels over the field and asks where the changing rooms are and if they can eat their lunch early, I go up to Sam. "I think I know what I have to do."

Sam slings her bag over her shoulder and waits.

I lower my voice so no one else can hear. I take a breath. This isn't as easy to say as I thought it would be. I've been dreaming of playing in a real

stadium all my life. It would have been awesome to be on that field. I'm about to

volunteer to kick my
dream into touch.

But Sam's right. "I'm not playing in the match," I tell her, "because I'd be stopping one of the real girls from getting a chance to play."

A smile spreads across Sam's face. "Congratulations." She hoists her bag further up her shoulder. "Now, come on, we've got an operation to get underway."

I put the small black box in place during a carefully timed bathroom break while Sam keeps lookout. I'm hoping the new gadgets from Mission Control are as good as they look. If I've read the instructions properly, the little black box I found is going to be even more effective than the disrupter.

Then we deliver the film to Mrs. Harrison, and all that's left to do is wait. And tell Mr. Caulfield that he needs a new player. I wait until the St.

Colmer's team has arrived and the warm-ups begin. A few people are filing through to take their seats.

"Mr. Caulfield?"

"Yes, Josie?"

"I'm sorry, sir, but I can't play today."

"What?"

"I was just warming up and I turned my ankle, sir. It really, really hurts." I pinch the inner skin of my wrist to make my eyes well up and make my mouth tremble as if I'm about to cry.

Then Sam comes running up as arranged. "Evie can play, Mr. Caulfield. She's a really good alternate and she's already wearing her uniform."

"I know who the alternates are, Sam," Mr. Caulfield says.

You can see him wondering if this is something to worry about. He shrugs. I think he's decided he's got enough to worry about already.

"Go and rest your ankle then, Josie."

I get myself out of the way, whispering "Good luck" to Sam.

She mouths, "You, too," and gives me a thumbs up.

I make my way into the stands and find a seat at the end of an aisle. Mr. Caulfield blows a whistle and the two teams run out onto the field.

From the start, it's clear that the visiting team has no chance. Evie is dominant on the ball and passes it to Sam four times in the first ten minutes. Sam scores—once on the first try, sneaking it into the left corner of the goal, and then again at the third chance by booting it straight past the opposition's goalie. The school goes wild after the second goal.

You have to give St. Colmer's credit for trying. They manage to get possession of the ball and kick it upfield. But then Sam darts up the field, cuts in, and takes it back to where it belongs—in goal. The score is three–zero to us! I'm not even sure Dan McGuire could score this many goals. Well, okay, maybe he could, but he's got the advantage of not being real.

A man next to me shakes his head. "They're very good for a girls' team."

I glare at him. "They're just incredible. Period."

"No, no, of course, yes, that's right, they are." The man coughs.

Finally, the whistle blows for half-time. It's time for the last stage of Operation Numbered to get underway.

Mrs. Harrison appears carrying a microphone and nearly trips as she sets it up. Really, I should have loaned her the stylus issue mic that Dad showed me. Full stadium coverage in a brooch or tie clip you can fasten to your shirt or jacket.

Mrs. Harrison taps the microphone and clears her throat. "Ladies and gentlemen, girls and boys. We are delighted to be here in order to raise funds for a very special cause, one that is close to the hearts of all those at Bothen Hill School."

Close to our hearts? Close to Mr. Caulfield's wallet more like.

"The job of telling you about Start Sports, the charity we are all here to support, has been taken on by two enterprising and creative young girls at our school, Sam and Josie. They kindly volunteered to make a special film about Start Sports so that you can all see where your donations have gone."

The crowd of parents and friends of the schools gives her a round of applause.

Mrs. Harrison smiles and gestures to the screen. "So, without further ado, let's find out all about Start Sports!"

I crane my neck to see Mr. Caulfield. He's taken a seat a few rows up from me. He's looking pretty relaxed, probably because he figures he'll be safely far away soon. Not soon enough, though.

Maybe I shouldn't say so myself but the film is completely professional. When we get to the part where Mr. Caulfield says the Chief Executive of the charity is Lesley Clock, it cuts away to a shot of the Start Sports' official list of employees. Then it slowly zooms in on the only name on the list: Mr. Caulfield.

There's a gasp from everyone in the stands, but the film's already moved on to the bank statements—zooming in on the name at the top again and again: Mr. Caulfield, Mr. Caulfield, Mr. Caulfield.

Operation Numbered is accomplished. As a bonus, I finally know how Dan McGuire feels when he's finished a mission. Awesome. Absolutely awesome.

It's not quite over, though, because Mr. Caulfield decides to make a run for it. Not that he can run very far. Or very fast. For a soccer coach, he's really out of shape.

It doesn't matter how fast he is anyway because we're ready for him. As he crosses the field, I take out the remote for the small black box I've installed near the exit. As Mr. Caulfield tries to go through I flip the first switch. A trip wire springs up, making Mr. Caulfield stumble. I flip the second switch. The box releases a wide net that drops over Mr. Caulfield and then clicks into place at his ankles.

"That's very clever." Sam appears at my side. "What about the police?"

I point over at Mrs. Harrison. She is jabbering into her cell phone and waving her free arm around.

"Won't they wonder where that net came from?" Sam asks.

"Oh don't worry about that. It's designed to dissolve after about twenty minutes. By the time the police get here there will be nothing left."

"Where *did* that net come from?"

"My dad works in security." It's *kind* of true.

"Okay." Sam punches me in the upper arm. "Anyway, well done, Josie. That wasn't bad at all . . ." She lowers her voice to a whisper, ". . . for a *boy*."

Chapter 17

Watching Mr. Caulfield being taken away by the police is completely awesome. He keeps trying to blame other people. At one point he even says it was all Mrs. Harrison's idea. Which is pretty stupid considering Mrs. Harrison was in charge of screening our documentary.

As arranged, Sam does all the talking to the police about the film. She's even agreed to say we "found" the papers. Since her mom is being promised a raise and promotion to chief reporter because of the story, she's really happy.

The only tricky part is when I have to go home and tell Mom and Dad what's happened. Even though I've finally got proof that I can be a good spy, I can't be sure how they'll take it. So, I talk fast and try to skim over the times where I nearly got caught. The only part I leave out is Sam knowing the truth about my cover. She's promised she won't tell anyone, and I trust her. And there's no point adding to Mom and Dad's stress levels.

After I've finished, there's this long pause. They're both looking their most spy-like. Dad stares at all the equipment I borrowed that I've put on the table. Mom stares at Dad.

"How did he get a hold of all of this, Jed?"

"You knew I was showing him around."

"You weren't supposed to show him the entry code!"

"I didn't!"

Some parents argue about the dishes. My parents argue about who's let the Mission Control pass code slip.

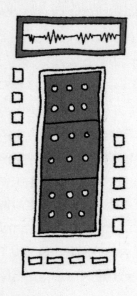

"It's not Dad's fault. I spied on him," I tell them.

They both swivel around to look at me.

"What? It's just what you do all the time!"

Dad laughs. "Genes win out, Zelia."

Mom shakes her head but she's smiling. "I suppose it ended well."

"We're proud of you." Dad says. "But next time, *ask* before you borrow." He picks up the recording Wite-Out and taps the lid. "It's expensive stuff."

"There's not going to be a next time," Mom says. "From now on we're playing by the book and *staying in the background.*"

Staying in the background works up until Sam comes over. I've told Mom and Dad that I have to be able to have a friend over now and then to cope with my cover. Dad answers the door.

"Hello, Mr. Marcus, Mrs. Marcus."

"Please. Call me . . ." Dad stops. His face looks blank and then takes on a look of panic. I guess he's still a bit thrown by everything I've told him.

"Oh, it's all right. I know they're not your real names anyway," Sam says.

There's a silence. Sam smiles cheerfully at them.

"Excuse me?" Dad looks from Sam to me, and back again.

I shake my head to show it's nothing to do with me.

"Don't worry," Sam says. "I won't tell anyone."

"Tell them what, Sam?" Mom sits down on the sofa.

"That the three of you are spies."

Sam thinks I'm a real spy!

"What?!" Mom sits bolt upright, her eyes fixed on Sam's face.

"I only guessed because I've gotten to know Josie so well. Nobody else would know. And anyway—a recording soccer ball, pen, and ruler? A device that sets off burglar alarms and fireworks? A remote-controlled trip wire and net?"

"I do work in security, Sam," Dad says.

"With a net that *dissolves*?"

"Jed . . ." Mom's voice is very low, with a hum of menace in it. "You said that we'd be *one hundred percent* safe."

"We are!" he says. Then he looks down. "We were."

"Honestly, don't worry. I won't tell anyone," Sam says again.

"I really can't tell you how important it is that you don't." Mom gives Sam her best Serious Spy look. She's obviously given up on denying it.

"Sure."

"So, what do we do now?" Mom runs her hand through her hair, looking worried. "Maybe we should ask HQ to leave earlier than planned. It's not fair to ask Sam to keep such a big secret."

"Oh, it's no problem. I'm good at it, aren't I, Josie?"

I grin at her. They have no idea how good.

"And anyway," Dad says, "we haven't finished *our* operation yet, Zelia."

"We could help," Sam says.

We all look at her.

"I mean, we did really well with Mr. Caulfield, didn't we? Why can't Josie and I do more jobs like that?"

"That's an *awesome* idea!" I say.

"All right, Josie." Mom shoots me a *that's enough* look.

"Come on, Mom. You've got to admit, no one will ever suspect two *kids*."

Mom and Dad look at each other, first in shock. Then the shock melts into something else—a sense of thinking it over, of possibility.

Dan McGuire, secret agent, spy genius, is fiction. But maybe Josie, undercover boy, secret spy, is about to become fact.

It might just make it worth being her for a bit longer.

Won't it?

Coming Soon

Spies in Disguise

Boy in a Tutu

To keep his family safe, Joe must still convince
the world he is "Josie." At least his life is
more fun now that Sam knows his secret,
and when they discover a plot, they must put
their spy skills to the test.

The new mission? To go undercover
in the dance school and find out what the
mysterious Mrs. Rushka is up to.

But Joe's mortified to discover that he'll be
playing the female lead! Can he keep it together
long enough to unmask the villain?